"You Said Sex Can Be Simple."

Nick peered at Brooke with assessing eyes, his gaze flowing over her lacy white gown that bared more cleavage and legs than she'd ever let him see before.

He swung his legs off the bed and stood. "It can be."

He looked like sex personified in a pair of jeans and nothing else. His body tight and muscled, his skin a golden-bronze.

"I need simple, Nick. With you."

He walked over to her and took the wine bottle from her hand. "You want to tell me what changed your mind?"

She closed her eyes. "No."

He set the wine bottle down and then the glasses. "I've been waiting for you," he said, then brushed his lips to hers gently, teasing, stroking with his tongue until she whimpered his name.

D1413369

Dear Reader,

When I began writing Nick Carlino's story for
NAPA VALLEY VOWS, I knew I wanted my reckless
"ladies' man" to find love, not only with the heroine,
but with a small child, as well. Having been born of a
ruthless father, Nick is the ultimate bachelor, leaving the
pursuits of fatherhood to his two other brothers.

But a midnight car crash in the hills of Napa and a
promise made change all that the minute Nick is reunited
with his high school friend Brooke Hamilton and her
sweet baby, Leah.

I've been moonlighting as a childbirth educator in a
local hospital for many years and I love all things
"baby." So writing this story was a complete joy for
me. I have to admit I fell in love with baby Leah first
and I think you will, too. Add a hunky reluctant hero
into the mix and a determined woman struggling not
to fall for wealthy Nick Carlino again, and we have
The Billionaire's Baby Arrangement.

I'm sorry to leave Napa Valley with this third and final
book, but I promise you an enjoyable read. In fact, it's
my solemn vow!

Cheers!

Charlene Sands

CHARLENE SANDS

THE BILLIONAIRE'S BABY ARRANGEMENT

Published by Silhouette Books
America's Publisher of Contemporary Romance

If you purchased this book without a cover you should be aware
that this book is stolen property. It was reported as "unsold and
destroyed" to the publisher, and neither the author nor the
publisher has received any payment for this "stripped book."

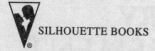

SILHOUETTE BOOKS

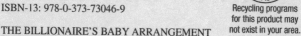

ISBN-13: 978-0-373-73046-9

Recycling programs
for this product may
not exist in your area.

THE BILLIONAIRE'S BABY ARRANGEMENT

Copyright © 2010 by Charlene Swink

All rights reserved. Except for use in any review, the reproduction
or utilization of this work in whole or in part in any form by any
electronic, mechanical or other means, now known or hereafter
invented, including xerography, photocopying and recording, or in
any information storage or retrieval system, is forbidden without
the written permission of the editorial office, Silhouette Books,
233 Broadway, New York, NY 10279 U.S.A.

This is a work of fiction. Names, characters, places and incidents are
either the product of the author's imagination or are used fictitiously, and
any resemblance to actual persons, living or dead, business establishments,
events or locales is entirely coincidental.

This edition published by arrangement with Harlequin Books S.A.

For questions and comments about the quality of this book please contact us
at Customer_eCare@Harlequin.ca.

® and TM are trademarks of Harlequin Books S.A., used under license.
Trademarks indicated with ® are registered in the United States Patent
and Trademark Office, the Canadian Trade Marks Office and in other
countries.

Visit Silhouette Books at www.eHarlequin.com

Printed in U.S.A.

Books by Charlene Sands

Silhouette Desire

The Heart of a Cowboy #1488
Expecting the Cowboy's Baby #1522
Like Lightning #1668
Heiress Beware #1729
Bunking Down with the Boss #1746
Fortune's Vengeful Groom #1783
Between the CEO's Sheets #1805
The Corporate Raider's Revenge #1848
*Five-Star Cowboy #1889
*Do Not Disturb Until Christmas #1906
*Reserved for the Tycoon #1924
Texan's Wedding-Night Wager #1964
†Million-Dollar Marriage Merger #2016
†Seduction on the CEO's Terms #2027
†The Billionaire's Baby Arrangement #2033

*Suite Secrets
†Napa Valley Vows

CHARLENE SANDS

Award-winning author Charlene Sands writes bold, passionate, heart-stopping heroes and always…really good men! She's a lover of all things romantic, having married her high school sweetheart, Don. She is the proud recipient of the Readers' Choice Award and double recipient of the Booksellers' Best Award, having written twenty-eight romances to date, both contemporary and historical Western. Charlene is a member of Romance Writers of America and belongs to the Orange County and Los Angeles Chapters of RWA, where she volunteers as the Published Authors Liaison.

When not writing, she loves movie dates with her hubby, playing cards with her children, reading romance, great coffee, Pacific beaches, country music and anything chocolate. She also loves to hear from her readers. You can reach Charlene at www.charlenesands.com or P.O. Box 4883, West Hills, CA 91308. You can find her on eHarlequin's Silhouette Desire Blog and on Facebook, too!

To Jason and Lindsay and Nikki and Zac.
May your lives always be filled with love, devotion and
joy. The four of you have made our family complete.
Here's to pizza dinners and game nights,
friendly competitions and traditions.

One

Nick Carlino hopped into his Ferrari and drove out of the Rock and A Hard Place parking lot, gravel crunching under his tires as he turned onto the road that led him to his Napa Valley home. He could really use a smoke right now and cursed the day he quit for good. Rachel Mancini had had that look in her eyes tonight, the one that told him she was getting serious. He'd seen that soft half-lidded expression a dozen times in the women he'd dated and each time he'd been wise enough to back off and let them down easily.

Nick liked Rachel. She was pretty and made him laugh and as the owner of the successful bar and nightclub, she intrigued him with her business smarts. He respected her and that's why Nick had to break it off with her. Rachel dropped hints like bombshells lately that she needed more. Nick didn't have more to give.

Moonlight guided his way on the dark patch of highway with vineyard columns on either side of him, the pungent scent of merlot and zinfandel grapes heavy in the summer air. He'd been called back to Napa after his father's death to help his two brothers run Carlino Wines and according to the will they had six months to decide which of Santo Carlino's three sons would become head of the empire. None of his old man's sons wanted the honor. So it was win by default. Yet Tony, Joe and Nick had pulled it together for the past five months and they had one more to figure out who'd run the company.

As Nick rounded a hilly curve, oncoming headlights beamed straight at him. He let out a loud curse. The car skidded halfway into his lane as it took the turn. Those beams hit him straight in the eyes and he swerved to avoid a head-on collision, but not enough to avoid impact. The two cars collided with a loud smack and his Ferrari whipped around in a tailspin. The jolt jarred him and his airbag deployed. He found himself sitting at a perpendicular angle to the car he'd just collided with.

"Damn," he muttered, barely getting the words out. Pressure from the air bag crushed his chest. He scooted his seat far back and then took a deep breath. Once he was sure all of his body parts were in working order, Nick got out of the car to check on the other driver.

The first thing he heard was a baby crying. Holy crap, he thought, fear gripping him tight. He moved quickly, glancing at the damage to the dated silver Toyota Camry as he strode past. He peered inside the car to find a woman behind the wheel, her body slumped forward, her head against the steering wheel. He opened the door with caution and saw blood dripping down her face.

The baby's cries grew louder. Nick opened the back door and glanced inside. The baby was in a car seat facing backward and looked to be okay—no blood anywhere, thank goodness. The car seat had done its job.

"Hang on, kid."

Nick didn't have a clue how old the child was, not an infant, but not yet at the walking stage, he presumed. He focused his attention on the woman behind the wheel, placing his hand on her shoulder. "Can you hear me? I'm getting help."

When she didn't respond, Nick braced her head and shoulders and gently guided her back, so that he could see her injuries. Blood oozed down her forehead—she had a deep gash from hitting the steering wheel. He rested her head back against the headrest.

Her eyes opened slowly and the first thing Nick noticed was the incredible hue of her hazel eyes. They were a mix of turquoise and green. He'd only seen that spectacular color once in his life. He brushed aside blond wisps of hair from her face, "Brooke? Brooke Hamilton, is that you?"

"My baby," she whispered, straining to get the words out, her eyes beginning to close again. "Take care of my baby."

"She's fine."

This woman he'd known in high school, twelve, maybe thirteen years ago, implored with her last conscious breath. "Promise me, you'll take care of Leah."

Without thinking, Nick agreed. "I promise I'll take care of her. Don't worry."

Brooke's eyes closed as she slipped out of her conscious world.

Nick dialed 9-1-1.

When he was through with the call, Nick got into the backseat of the car. The baby's sobs grew to soft whimpers that tore at Nick's heart. "I'm coming, kid. I'll get you outta this contraption."

Nick could write a book about what he didn't know about babies. He had no idea how to remove the little girl from the straps that bound her into the car seat—hell, he'd never even held a baby before. He struggled for a minute, then finally figured out the release, all the while muttering soft words to the helpless child.

To his amazement, the baby stopped crying and looked up at him, her face flushed and her breaths slowing. With eyes wide, she stared at him in wonderment with her mother's big hazel eyes. "You're gonna break hearts with those eyes," he said softly.

The baby's lips curled up. The smile caught him by surprise.

Nick lifted her out of the car seat, holding her awkwardly in his arms. "You need someone who knows about babies," he said quietly.

Nick shifted the baby onto one arm and got his cell phone out again to call Rena, Tony's wife. She'd know what to do, then he remembered the late hour and how much trouble Rena was having sleeping these days. She was nearly ready to have her own baby. He clicked off before the phone had a chance to ring and dialed Joe's number. Joe's fiancée, Ali, would come running to help and he'd be glad to turn the baby over to her tonight.

The phone went straight to voicemail. Nick left a quick message then remembered Ali and Joe were vacationing in the Bahamas this week. "Great," he muttered, taking the baby in both of his arms now. "Looks like it's me and you. That's not good news for you, kid."

Before the paramedics arrived, Nick managed to sift through the woman's handbag and find her driver's license. In the car's dim overhead light, he saw he wasn't wrong. The woman who'd swerved into his lane and caused the accident was Brooke Hamilton-Keating. He'd gone to high school with her. He'd gone further than high school with her once, but that was ancient history.

Nick sat the baby down on the backseat. "Sh, you be quiet now, okay? I've gotta check on your mama."

The second he released her, she whimpered.

Nick gazed at her and made a slow move toward Brooke. The baby opened her mouth and let out a wail.

"Okay, fine." Nick picked her up again and as soon as she was back in his arms, she quieted. "Let's both see to your mama."

Nick held the baby in one arm and opened the front passenger door. He slid in carefully and adjusted the baby in his right arm, so he could look Brooke over better than he had before. She was out cold, but still breathing. He didn't think the collision had been enough to cause internal injuries, but hell, he was no doctor so he couldn't be sure.

Sirens in the distance sent a wave of relief through him. Nick closed his eyes for a moment. It was late and no other cars were on the road. Napa wasn't exactly a party town and the road they were on led to nothing but residential properties and vineyards.

With the baby in his arms, Nick greeted two paramedics in dark blue uniforms that came bounding out of the van. "The baby seems fine, but the mother is unconscious," he said.

"What happened, sir?" one of them asked.

"One minute I'm driving around a curve, the next this Camry is coming at me head on. I swerved the second I saw her car, or it could have been a lot worse."

"The baby yours or hers?" he asked as he examined Brooke.

"Hers."

He looked at his partner. "We'll take them both to the

hospital." Then he turned to Nick. "How about you? Are you injured?"

"No. The air bag inflated and I'm fine. The Camry doesn't have one, apparently."

The paramedic nodded. "Looks like the car seat saved the baby any injuries."

Within fifteen minutes, the police arrived to take a statement and Brooke's gurney was hoisted into the ambulance. Nick stood by, holding Leah in his arms.

"I'll take her now," the paramedic said, reaching for the baby.

"What'll they do with her?"

"Give her a full exam and then try to reach a relative."

The second Leah was out of Nick's arms, she put up a big fuss. Her face turned red and those big eyes closed as she wailed loud enough to wake the dead. Worse yet, when she opened her eyes, she stared straight at Nick looking at him as if he were her savior.

He remembered the promise he made to her mother.

"Let me have her," he said, reaching for the baby. "I'll ride with you to the hospital."

The paramedic cast him a skeptical look and kept Leah with him.

"I know the mother. We went to high school together. I promised her I'd watch out for Leah."

"When?"

"She opened her eyes and was conscious long enough to make sure the baby was taken care of."

The paramedic sighed. "She likes you a heck of lot better than me. Grab the diaper bag in the car and anything else you see they might need. We've got to get going."

Brooke opened her eyes slowly and even that slight movement caused a slashing pain across her forehead. She reached up to rub it and found a bandage there. She didn't know how long she'd been out, but slivers of sunshine warmed her body.

Her first thought was of Leah and a wave of panic gripped her. "Leah!"

She sat straight up abruptly and her head spun. Her eyes rolled back and she nearly lost consciousness again.

Stay awake, Brooke.

She fought dizziness and took slow, deep breaths.

"She's here," a masculine voice announced softly.

Brooke glanced in the direction of the voice, narrowing her eyes to focus. She saw Leah tucked into her pink blanket, looking peaceful and content, sleeping in the arms of a man. Relief swamped her at first. Her beautiful baby was safe. Tears sprung from her eyes when fragments of the accident played over in her head. She'd gotten distracted by Leah's wailing as she navigated a sharp curve in the road. She glanced back for an instant to check on her and the next thing she knew, she'd collided with another car. She vaguely remembered waking for a moment before all had gone black. Brooke took a minute to thank God for keeping Leah safe in the Peg Perego car seat she'd insisted on when she was pregnant.

Her gaze shifted up to the deep blue eyes and self-assured smile of... Nick Carlino? She'd never forgotten the timbre of his voice that oozed sex or the handsome sharp angles of his face. Or the dimples that jumped out when he smiled. It was enough to make a girl get naked in just under a minute.

She knew. She'd been one of those girls, way back when.

Oh, God.

"Leah is safe," he assured her again.

That's all that mattered to her. "Nick Carlino?"

"It's me, Brooke." Those dimples peeked out for a moment.

She reached out for Leah and the movement rattled pain through her head. "I want to hold my baby."

"She's sleeping," he said, not moving a muscle.

Brooke rested her head against her pillow. It was probably better she didn't wake Leah now, she still felt light-headed. "Is she really okay?"

"She was examined last night. The doctor said she had no injuries."

"Thank God," Brooke whispered, tears once again stinging her eyes. "But why are you here?" She couldn't wrap her head around why Nick was holding her baby in her hospital room.

"You really don't remember?"

"I barely know my own name at the moment."

"You came around a turn late last night and crashed into my car. For a minute there, I thought it was lights out for all of us."

"It was your car I hit?" If she were a cruel-hearted woman she'd say it was poetic justice.

"My *Ferrari*. Yeah."

His *Ferrari*. Of course. Nick always had to have the best of everything. How was she ever going to pay for the repairs? She'd let her insurance lapse when she took off from Los Angeles.

"I'm sorry. I don't know what happened."

"What were you doing driving so late at night?"

"I was looking for my aunt's place and must have taken a wrong turn. The roads were dark and I got distracted. We'd been driving all day and I'd thought we could make it to her place rather than stop at a motel for the night. Are you all right? You weren't injured, were you?"

She still couldn't believe that Nick Carlino was in her

hospital room, holding her baby in his arms like Leah belonged there. A shudder went through her. This was all so surreal.

"I'm fine. The air bag saved my as—uh, butt."

She let go a sigh. "Oh, that's good. What about your car?"

"Needs some repairs."

"And mine?"

"The same. I had them towed to my mechanic's shop."

Brooke wouldn't think about the cost to repair those cars. If she did, the tremors in her head would escalate to a major earthquake.

"You haven't been here all night?" she asked.

The dimples of doom came out on cue and he gave a short nod. Her heart fluttered. "You have?"

He glanced down at Leah then up at her again. "I promised you I'd take care of her last night."

"You did?"

"You were adamant, Brooke. You woke just for a minute to make sure Leah was taken care of. You made me promise."

"Thank you," she said, holding back another round of tears. She didn't need to fall apart in front of Nick Carlino. "I appreciate all you did last night for my baby."

Nick nodded and glanced down at Leah for a second. "Where's her father?"

Brooke blinked. Leah's father, Dan? The man she'd been married to for all of two years, who had told her on her twenty-ninth birthday that he was having an affair with a woman he'd always loved and that he'd gotten her pregnant? He'd left Brooke that night, and one week later she found out that she herself was going to have a baby. That father?

"He's not in the picture."

"Not at all?"

Nick seemed amazed by this. Didn't he know how many deadbeat dads there were in this world? Her own father left her mother when Brooke was six years old. She'd rarely seen him, but when he did come around, Brooke would cling to him very tight and beg him to stay longer. He never did. "Daddy's got to go," her mother would say. Brooke never understood why Daddy couldn't live with her any longer. And she cried for him, night after night, praying he'd come home to stay. After she turned ten, he never came around again.

Brooke wouldn't subject little Leah to that heartache and pain. She'd moved away from Los Angeles and Dan, and spent the next months living on her own, managing a small seaside inn on the California coast just outside of San Diego. The little beach town fit her needs at the time. It paid the bills and she liked the cool ocean breezes and smog-free sunshine. It was good for her pregnancy and good for her state of mind.

"No, Dan's not in the picture at all." It felt good saying it. She knew one day she'd have to tell Dan about Leah, but not now. Not yet. She needed to get Aunt Lucy's place up and running and making money before she'd tell Dan about his child. She needed all the ammunition she could get to retain full custody of Leah. That's if Dan would even want his daughter. But Brooke couldn't take any chances. She'd inherited her aunt's eight-bedroom home in Napa Valley and with a little ingenuity she planned to make the place a shining bed-and-breakfast for tourists.

"So, you're visiting your aunt?" Nick asked matter-of-factly, as if he'd already come to that conclusion.

"My aunt passed on three months ago. I inherited her home."

When Nick was ready to pose another question, Leah fidgeted in his arms and made sweet little waking-up sounds. Nick stiffened, appearing confused as to what to do with her.

"She's hungry and probably wet."

On impulse, Nick moved her away from his body, looking at her bottom through the blanket. "You think so?"

"Has she been in the same diaper all night?"

"Yes, no. I think one of the nurses changed her late last night and fed her." He pointed to her suitcases at the other end of the room. "She found what she needed in there."

"Oh, I hadn't even thought about my things. Did you bring them here last night?"

He nodded and stood. She moved her eyes up the length of him and inhaled a steady breath of air. His day-old stubble and wrinkled clothes made Nick look even more appealing, sexier than she'd remembered. She found that he'd filled out his boyish frame to one of a man who could sustain every woman's fantasy.

Good thing he was leaving. "I'll take Leah now. I'm sure I'll be on my way soon," she said.

The doctor walked in at that very moment with a chart in his hands. "I wouldn't be too sure of that." He introduced himself as Dr. Maynard.

Blood drained from her face and her insides knotted. "Why not?"

"While your tests show no damage, you took one nasty bump to the head. You're going to have bouts of dizziness. You won't be able to drive and it's better that you rest for at least two days."

The doctor did a cursory exam, removing the bandage on her head, nodding that it looked better. He checked her eyes with a probing light and used his stethoscope to listen to her heart. "I can release you today into someone's care, though. Do you have help for your baby?"

She shook her head. "I just arrived in town last night."

And what an entrance she'd made. "I can call a friend." She'd kept in contact with Molly Thornton for several years after she'd graduated from high school. Though she hadn't spoken with Molly in two years, she knew she'd lend a hand if needed. Molly was the nurturing type and wouldn't let a friend down.

"Okay, I'll get your release ready. I'm writing you a prescription for pain relievers. Nothing too strong. Are you still nursing the baby?"

Brooke nodded. "Yes."

He glanced at Leah, who was kicking up more of a fuss now in Nick's arms. "She's cute. I have a daughter a few months older than her." Then he glanced at Nick. "I never thought I'd see a baby in *your* arms, Carlino." The doctor glanced back at Brooke. "Next time you come to Napa, I wouldn't suggest you crash into Nick." He winked at her. "It's safer to steer clear when you see him coming."

Brooke had already come to that conclusion, years ago.

Nick twisted his lips. "Funny, Maynard. But you won't be laughing when I kick your butt on the court Friday."

"Keep dreaming." Dr. Maynard turned back to Brooke, his serious face on. "Be sure to have someone pick you up today and stay with you. Take it easy for a few days."

"Okay, thank you, doctor."

When he left the room, she turned to Nick, who had calmed Leah down again. Leave it to Nick to know how to persuade a female. "I'll take Leah now."

Nick walked close to the bed, holding Leah like she was a football tucked close to his body. Her daughter stared at him with wide eyes.

"She seems to like me," he said, mystified. "I don't have a clue about babies. Until last night, I'd never held one in my arms."

"You never had children?"

"No little bambinos for me. I'm leaving that up to my brothers."

She glanced at his left hand looking for a wedding ring and when he caught her, she must have turned a shade of bright red judging by the heat creeping up her neck. Nick always had that effect on her. He'd turn her inside out and then leave her blushing, or worse. The one night they had together, he'd humiliated her so badly she thought she'd die from embarrassment. She must have been the locker room joke of the day for all the jocks on the Napa Valley Victors.

Baseball, girls and partying were Nick Carlino's claims to fame in high school.

Brooke had been crazy to think that Nick would have wanted her. The golden boy, the first baseman with a .450 hitting average, born with a silver spoon in his mouth and heading for great things—Brooke found out just how out of her league she'd been with him.

He'd nearly ruined her seventeen-year-old life. Her self-esteem had hit rock bottom and it had taken her years to recover. All of the negative things she'd believed about herself had been confirmed. And she'd hated him all the more for it.

Now, she glanced at him as he handed over her five-month-old baby. He was looking handsome and sinfully delicious, and she hated the slight trembles invading her stomach. The sooner she got away from him the better. She wanted no reminder of her past and wished she had crashed into anyone else on earth last night but Nick Carlino.

"It's simple, Brooke. You'll stay overnight at my house."

"I can't do that, Nick." Brooke put her stubborn face on

and refused to budge, ignoring the spinning in her head. While he was gone, she'd gotten up and dressed in the hospital room, made three phone calls to Molly to no avail, then nursed Leah on the same leather rocker Nick had sat watch on last night.

When Nick said a casual good-bye earlier, she'd known she'd still have to deal with him regarding the damages to his car, but she hadn't expected him to return to her hospital room two hours later.

She'd found him leaning against the doorjamb, staring at her while she nursed Leah, his lips pursed together in an odd expression. An intimate moment passed between them before he'd started issuing orders like a drill sergeant.

"I'll figure something out," she said quietly, not to disturb Leah. She always had before. She'd supported herself during her pregnancy and managed to deliver a baby without a partner so she could certainly handle this dilemma without a lot of fuss.

"Like what? You're out of options." He could be just as stubborn, she thought, watching him fold his arms over his chest and take a wide stance. "You can't reach your friend and you heard what the doctor said."

"I'll deal with it. Thank you. I don't need your help."

Nick sat down on a chair. Bracing both of his forearms on his knees, he leaned toward her. He looked deep into her eyes and his dark penetrating gaze blindsided her. "Wow, it's been what? Thirteen years, and you're still holding a grudge."

Brooke gasped and Leah stopped nursing. She settled her baby down and waited until she continued sucking, making sure to cover both the baby and her breast with the blanket.

She wanted to be anywhere but here, having this conversation with Nick. It amazed her that he even remembered that night. To her it was a mind-sucking, punched-in-the-gut experience, but she presumed it was business as usual for Nick. He'd probably left dozens of humiliated girls in his wake during his lifetime. "I'm not holding a grudge." It had been so much more than that for her. "I barely know you."

"You know me well enough to accept my help when you need it."

"I don't need it." Even to her ears she sounded contrary. "Why do you care anyway?"

Nick ran a hand through his dark hair and shook his head. "It's no big deal, Brooke. I live in a huge house, practically by myself. You'll stay a night or two and my conscience will be clear."

"You're worried about your conscience?" That sounded like the Nick Carlino she'd known, the one who watched out for Numero Uno first and foremost.

"I promised to take care of Leah last night. And her mother needs a quiet place to rest. Dammit, maybe I'm just sorry I didn't swerve outta your way faster."

Brooke was losing this argument fast and that made her nervous. "You weren't the one in the wrong lane. It's my fault. Besides, who's going to look after us, you?"

Nick shrugged. "I'll hire a nurse for a few days. We'd probably never see each other."

"I can't afford that."

"I can," Nick said point-blank. Not in the cocky way he had about him either. He seemed sincere.

The idea sounded better and better to her, yet how could she accept his charity?

He was right about one thing—she was out of options. With the exception of Molly, she'd broken all ties with her friends from Napa Valley when her mother moved them away right after graduation.

Brooke had never felt like she fit in with the sons and daughters of wealthy winegrowers, landowners and old Napa money. She was one of a handful of students at the school that wasn't of the privileged class. Her mother managed the Cabernet Café down the street from the high school and Brooke had worked there after school and on weekends. It had started out being a wine-tasting room, but after it failed the owner changed the place into a burger and shake joint. The kids at school called it the Cab Café and the name stuck.

When Brooke didn't answer, Nick landed the final blow. "Think about what your daughter needs."

She squeezed her eyes shut momentarily. God. He was right. Leah needed a healthy mother. Having a nurse on duty meant that Leah would be cared for and Brooke would get the rest she needed. Waves of light-headedness had come and gone all morning long. It was barely eleven and she was already exhausted. Every bone in her body seemed to ache at one time or another when she moved. The soreness she could handle, but she needed to be fully alert in caring for Leah.

Damn Nick. While she should be thanking him for his generous offer, she resented that he had the means to provide exactly what she needed. Why did it have to be Nick? It seemed like a very bad, cruel joke.

"Well?" he asked.

The idea of spending one minute under Nick Carlino's roof made her cringe.

"Just let me try calling Molly one more time."

Two

Nick glanced at Brooke sitting there on the passenger side of his Cadillac Escalade SUV. The only indication of the crash that took her to the hospital last night was the bandage on her forehead. "All set?" He leaned over to give an extra tug on her seat belt and met with her cautious eyes.

"Yes," she said, averting her gaze. After a moment of hesitation, she asked, "How did you get the car seat for Leah?"

Nick looked in the back seat where the baby lay resting against a lambswool cushion. "My mechanic, Randy, has two kids. He installed it for me."

"I think I'm supposed to get a new one now. After a crash, a car seat needs to be replaced."

"I didn't know that."

"How would you?"

"I wouldn't," he agreed, not missing Brooke's impatience. He figured her head ached more than she let on. Lines of fatigue crinkled her otherwise stunning eyes and she appeared exhausted. "My house isn't far."

"I guess we haven't got a choice."

We, meaning her and Leah. Nick caught her drift. "I'll drive slow to the House of Doom and Gloom."

Brooke glanced at him. "Is that what you call it?"

"Me? No. But you, on the other hand, look like you're going to your own execution."

Brooke faced him with a frown. "It just wasn't supposed to happen like this."

"What wasn't?"

"Me, coming back to Napa."

"What was supposed to happen?"

"I was supposed to reach my aunt's house by daylight. Walk in and find an immaculate house filled with antique furniture. Leah and I would spend the night and then in the morning, I'd be making plans to open it to the public."

"Guess what? Life doesn't always work out the way you planned."

"That's cynical, coming from you."

Nick started the engine. "Because I'm wealthy and entitled, right?"

Brooke sighed and blew breath from her heart-shaped mouth. Nick didn't dwell on that mouth. If he did, he'd be knee-deep in babies and beautiful blondes with attitude. He was simply being a Good Samaritan here. But it irked him that Brooke thought it so out of character for him to help her.

"Nice car. Whose is it?"

Nick blinked at her rapid change of subject. "Mine."

She smiled, though he saw what that curling of her lips cost her pain-wise. "I make my point."

Instead of being irritated, Nick chuckled. He hadn't seen that coming. He liked a good sparring partner and

Brooke had just surprised him. "So you think because I drive nice cars and live in a big house, I have everything that I want?"

"Don't you?"

Nick shook his head. He didn't have to think twice. "No." He'd wanted something more than all those things and he'd lost it, just when it was within his grasp. "Not everything, Brooke."

He sensed her gaze on him for a few long seconds and then she laid her head against the headrest and closed her eyes, which gave him a chance to really look at her. Unfortunately, he liked what he saw. Silken lashes framed almond-shaped eyes and rested on cheekbones that were high and full. He'd already decided he liked her mouth. He'd kissed her before, but the image of those kisses had blurred with age.

Long, wavy blond locks tumbled down her shoulders and rested on the soft full mounds of her breasts. Her body was shapely, but he'd never have guessed she'd had a child five months ago from her slim waistline and flat stomach.

Don't go there, Nick warned. He wasn't the fatherly type. He had zero plans to get tied down with a family. His past haunted him daily and reminded him that he was better off single, glorying in bachelorhood than trying his hand at anything more.

He drove the car slowly as promised and made his way onto the highway. "Where's your aunt's place?"

"Just outside of the city on Waverly Drive."

Nick knew the area. It was at the base of the foothills, before the roads led to higher ground and the bulk of the vineyards. "You want to do a drive-by?"

Her eyes widened, lighting up her face. "Yes."

"You're up to it?" he asked, wondering if he should have suggested it.

"I am. I'm curious to see what the place looks like. It's been years since I've seen it."

"You never came back to Napa? Even though you had an aunt living here?"

"No," she said. "I never came back."

Nick looked at her and she once again averted her eyes by looking out the window.

They drove in silence the rest of the way.

Brooke didn't want to tell him that her Aunt Lucy was her father's sister. That after her parents' marriage broke up, her mother never talked to Aunt Lucy again. But her aunt would sneak visits to Brooke, coming around after school to walk her partway home. When Brooke was in high school, Aunt Lucy would ask her to stop by the house. Brooke had little family and she liked Aunt Lucy, even if she was a bit eccentric. Eventually, her mother found out about the visits but she never tried to stop them.

When they moved away, Brooke had fully intended to keep in touch with her aunt, but time had gotten away from her. She'd always feel guilty that she hadn't made more of an effort to see her aunt before she died. Inheriting her house had come as a bolt from the blue and there'd been only one stipulation in the will, that Brooke not sell the place for a period of five years. With her mother remarried and living in Hawaii, it only made sense for Brooke to come back and try to build a life here for Leah and herself.

She glanced at Nick, who'd just taken a turn off the highway. He was part of the reason she'd never wanted to come back here. Thirteen years had dulled the pain and she'd almost forgotten that deep sense of rejection—of not being good enough, of falling for the wrong boy and feeling like a fool, but then fate had a way of intervening and turning Brooke's life upside down.

She'd managed to crash into the very man she'd wanted to avoid at all costs. And now she was his charity case. She was going to live under his roof, accept his help and be beholden to him for the rest of eternity.

Good going, Brooke.

"What's the address?" Nick turned onto Waverly Drive and looked at her for direction.

"It's up half a block on your right. It's the only three-story house on the street."

The houses were sparsely spaced, each parcel of land at least half an acre. If Brooke remembered correctly, her aunt owned slightly more acreage than her neighbors. In fact, it was by far the largest piece of land in the vicinity.

"It's there," Brooke said, pointing to the lot she remembered. Eager anticipation coursed through her veins and excitement bubbled up. This was the start of her new life. She remembered driving up here in her beat-up 1984 Chevy Caprice when she was in high school. "The Victorian that looks like…" she began and a sense of doom crept into her gut. Her heart sank. The wrought iron gates that were once pearly white grabbed the sunlight with golden hues of rust and age. The flower garden once bright with pansies, daffodils and lavender was a mass of weeds and as Nick drove into the driveway that led to the house, Brooke's heart sank even further. The house looked like something from an Addams Family television reunion, the only thing missing were the cobwebs. And Brooke even thought she saw a few of those tangled up on the third story.

"Oh," she said, tears welling in her eyes. "It's not like I remembered."

Nick glanced at her. "Do you want to go inside?"

"I should. Might as well face the music." She smiled with

false bravado. What had she expected? Her aunt had been ill for the last few years of her life. Obviously, maintaining the house hadn't been high on her list of priorities. Another wave of guilt assaulted her. Had her aunt been alone when she died? Did she have anyone to sit by her bedside when she was ill?

She looked at Nick. "But Leah's asleep."

"I'll stay. You go in and check the place out."

When she debated it for a few seconds, Nick added, "Unless you want me to go inside with you?"

"No, no. That's not necessary. If you can watch Leah, I'll go in."

Nick got out of the car at the same time she did. He took her arm and led her up the steps. His touch and being so near as he walked with her mingled with all the other emotions clouding her head. She didn't want to owe him, but here he was, doing her a favor again. And touching her in a comforting way that led her mind to other touches, other days when Nick had surprised her with kindness, only to destroy her in one fell swoop. Today, even in her weakened state, she wouldn't let Nick's touch mean anything. She didn't trust him. Not in that way.

She stepped onto the wraparound porch by the front door and stood a moment, hesitating.

"Are you all right?" Nick asked, holding her arm tight.

"I'm fine. Just can't believe it."

Nick smiled and her heart rammed into her chest. "I'll be right out here. Call if you need me."

She removed his hand from her arm and stepped back.

Nick looked at her skeptically, but bounded down the steps and stood watch over Leah, sleeping in her car seat.

She turned toward the front door and reached into her purse for the key.

Five minutes later, Brooke had seen all there was to see

and it wasn't pretty. The house had been let go for years. The only rooms that were in halfway decent shape were the kitchen and her aunt's bedroom. Those rooms looked somewhat cared for, but the others needed quite a bit of work. It would take a whole lot of elbow grease and some of her hard-saved cash to make it shine, and right now, the whole situation overwhelmed her.

She stood on the porch and found Nick leaning against the side of his car, the open door letting air inside for her daughter. "Well?"

"Let's just say the inside makes the outside look like Buckingham Palace."

"That bad?"

Brooke walked down the steps a little too fast and everything spun. She fought to keep her balance, wooziness swamping her. She swayed and was immediately caught. Nick's arms came around her. "Whoa."

Her body pressed against his. He was rock solid and strong, yet his arms around her were gentle. He pressed his hands to her back and rubbed. "Are you okay?"

"I will be as soon as you stop spinning me around."

He chuckled.

She clung to him, trying to find her balance. Breathing in his sexy musk scent wasn't helping matters. He felt too darn good. She hadn't had a man hold her like this for a year and a half. She'd been deprived of masculine contact for a long time. That was the only explanation for the warm sensations rippling through her body. She'd gotten over Nick Carlino ages ago.

"Bad idea," Nick said softly in her ear.

Oh God. She stiffened and backed away. Did he think she'd thrown herself at him? "I know."

"I shouldn't have suggested bringing you here. You're not up to it."

Stunned, Brooke didn't respond. Clearly, she'd taken his "bad idea" comment the wrong way. She could only look into his eyes and nod. "I think you're right. But I'm feeling okay now, the world's not spinning."

He took her hand and led her to the car. "C'mon. I'll get you home. You need to rest."

Brooke got into the car and closed her eyes the entire way to Nick's house. Partly to rest and partly to block out how good Nick felt when he held her close. He was solid and steady and caring. If he were any other man, she might have enjoyed the sensations skipping through her body, but since it was Nick, she warned them off. He'd been out of her league the first time and nothing had changed, except now she knew better than to take Nick Carlino seriously.

She rubbed her temples and adjusted the bandage, thinking fate had a great sense of humor.

Only Brooke didn't find any of this amusing.

She'd heard about the Carlino estate, driven past its massive grounds in her earlier years many times, but nothing in her wildest imaginings had prepared Brooke when she entered the home for the first time. While she expected opulence and cold austere surroundings, she found…warmth.

That was a shock.

The stone entryway led to rooms of creams and beiges, golden textured walls, rich wood beamed ceilings and living spaces filled with furniture that she would describe as comfortable elegance. A giant floor-to-ceiling picture window in the living room lent a view of lush grounds and vineyards below.

The architecture of the home was more villa style than anything else. It was an open plan on the first floor but the upstairs spread out to four separate wings, Nick explained.

He followed Brooke to the stairway, carrying her bags as she held Leah.

"You doing okay?" Nick asked from behind as she climbed the steps.

"Great, you won't have to catch me again."

"No, I'm not that lucky."

Was he flirting? Boy, she was struggling to keep her head from clouding up and one comment from him had her head spinning again.

When she reached the top of the stairs, she stopped and turned. "Which way?"

Nick stood on the step below her and their eyes met on the same level. He stared at her, then cast his gaze lower to where Leah had clutched her blouse, pulling the material aside enough to expose her bra. Nick flashed Brooke a grin, dimples and all, then looked back at Leah, who seemed absolutely fascinated with him. He poked her tiny nose gently and the baby giggled. "Go into the first set of double doors you see."

Brooke entered the room and then blurted, "This is your room."

She couldn't miss it. His baseball trophies sat on a shelf next to pictures of Nick with his brothers and one family photo from when both of his parents were alive. The entire room oozed masculinity from the hardwood floors covered with deep rust rugs and a quilt of the same color covering his king-size bed. Another picture window offered an amazing view of Napa from the hilltop.

"Yes. It's my room."

She whirled around and narrowed her eyes at him. "Surely, you don't expect..." She couldn't finish her sentence, her mind conjuring up hurtful images of the last time she'd been with Nick.

Nick set her bags down and leisurely looked her over

from the top of her bandaged head to her toes inserted in beach flip-flops. Tingles of panic slid through her.

"It makes the most sense, Brooke. There's an adjoining room where the nurse will sleep." And finally, he added, "I'll take the guest room, two doors down."

Her sigh of relief was audible and so embarrassing that she couldn't face him. What made her think he was at all interested in her anyway? He probably had scores of women dangling, just waiting for a call from him.

She scoured the room looking for a safe place to lay Leah down to sleep. Finally, she glanced at Nick, who was busy taking out a few items of clothing from his dresser. "There was a little play yard for Leah in the trunk of my car."

"It's here."

"It is?"

He nodded. "I got the rest of your things out of your trunk this morning."

"And you brought them here?"

He shrugged. "I figured the kid needed them. I'll bring them up later."

Overwhelmed with gratitude and ready to cry, she didn't know what to say. "I, uh…thank you, Nick."

"No problem. Use whatever you need. There's a great shower and tub. Climb into bed if you want to. The nurse is due in half an hour. I'll send her up when she gets here."

"What about you? You must have had plans today. Don't let us keep you."

"Sweetheart, no one keeps me from doing what I want to do." He winked and walked out of the bedroom.

How well she knew.

"Well, Leah, that was Nick Carlino."

Leah looked around, her eyes wide, fascinated by her new surroundings. She made a cooing sound that warmed Brooke's heart. All that mattered was that both of them were safe and provided for at the moment. She sat down on Nick's bed and bounced Leah on her knee. "Promise me you won't go falling for him, baby girl," she said, clapping their hands together and making Leah giggle. "He's not to be trusted. Mommy did that once and it wasn't good. Not good at all."

"That's a first for you," his brother Joe said, as he toweled off from his swim in the pool. "You're letting a woman and her child stay at the house."

"It's not like I had a choice." Nick glanced at his middle brother with disdain. "What was I supposed to do? She's got a kid. She's injured and has nowhere else to go. I couldn't walk away. Her head's not right."

"Must not be, if she moved in with you." Joe toweled off from his swim and put his glasses back on. He was building his fiancée a house and though he lived at Ali's condo currently, Nick had to put up with his gibes when he came over to do his hundred laps in the pool. Joe was the geek in the family and swimming was his only means of physical activity.

"Good thing you know your way around a computer. You'd never make it as a comedian."

Joe ignored him. "Who is she?"

"Her name is Brooke Hamilton. We went to high school together."

"Brooke Hamilton? That name sounds familiar."

Nick kept his mouth shut. Let his brother figure it out.

"Oh, she's the one who worked at that Cab Café, right?"

Bingo.

"I remember her now. She was the waitress who had a big crush on you."

"Ancient history." Nick didn't want to bring up the past.

It had been the one time in his young life he'd done the right thing. The one time, he'd put someone else's needs above his own. He'd let Brooke off the hook. Still, after all these years, when she looked at him, it was with wariness and contempt. Could it be she still held a grudge over what happened?

"So you're the Good Samaritan now?"

"Something like that," Nick muttered, squinting into the sun. "Like I said, she's here temporarily. A few days at most. Just until Maynard gives her the okay to be on her own."

"Yeah, speaking of that, how is it that my little brother gets in a car crash and doesn't tell his brothers?"

"I tried calling. Then I remembered you were in the Bahamas. Or were supposed to be."

"We got back late last night. If you got our voicemail, it's probably because we were sleeping. So, how are you?"

Nick lifted his arms out wide. "I'm gonna live."

"Amen to that, little brother. How old's the kid?"

"Leah is five months old."

"A baby?" Joe looked at him with suspicion. "You're not—"

Nick shook his head. "I just laid eyes on Brooke last night. I haven't seen her since high school. But thanks for the vote of confidence, bro."

"Hey, don't take offense," Joe said. "But you do have a reputation with the ladies."

Nick couldn't deny it. He liked women and they liked him back. They had a good time together and then Nick would let them down gently and walk away. Or they'd get fed up with not getting a commitment from him and leave on their own. He never led them on or lied to them. From the beginning, he'd always let the women in his life know what to expect from him. It had been that way since he could remember. As a young man, he assumed he'd grow out of it when the right woman came along, but his father had taken that option away from him in his attempt to control Nick. Santo Carlino had wanted one son to take over the family business and once Tony left to race cars and Joe took off to New York to develop software for a global company, the youngest son got the brunt of his father's manipulations.

Santo had done a number on him and Nick had taken a hard fall.

"I'm not interested in Brooke Hamilton. Hell, give me a break, Joe. I'm doing a good deed here, not looking for an instant family."

Damn it! Nick glanced up to find Brooke standing behind Joe. The baby bottle she held slipped from her hand. Flustered, her face turned color and Nick couldn't tell if she was angry or embarrassed.

Angry, he decided.

Joe swept up the bottle quickly and handed it to her. "Here you go. Hi, I'm Joe."

"I remember. Hi, Joe." She took the bottle graciously and smiled at him. Those knock-out hazel eyes, the shade of tropical waters, lit up her whole face.

"Sorry to hear about the accident," Joe said. "I hope you recover well from your injuries."

"Thank you." As if she had forgotten about her head injury, she touched her forehead. "I'm doing okay."

"Shouldn't you be resting?" Nick asked. He'd shown the nurse to their room an hour ago and she'd promised to watch over both mother and child.

She glanced at him and the light in her eyes faded as fast as her smile. "I couldn't calm down so I thought I'd get some air."

"With that?" Nick pointed to the baby's bottle. Seemed she only had a smile for Joe.

"Oh, I was on my way to the kitchen to store this. It's expressed breast milk."

Nick blinked. "Expressed?"

"I think this is my cue to leave," Joe said, adjusting the glasses on his nose. He darted glances at both of them then bid them good-bye and left.

"Sorry to bother you," Brooke said to him, not sounding sorry at all as she turned to leave.

"Brooke?"

She stopped and whirled around. "It's not as if Leah and I have a choice in this, Nick. I don't mean to sound ungrateful, but I don't want to be here anymore than you want us here."

"If I didn't want you here, you wouldn't be here. Why couldn't you calm down?"

Brooke fidgeted with the bottle in her hands. He didn't want to think about how she'd expressed the milk into the bottle. Some things were beyond male comprehension. She glanced away, looking at the pool, then the grounds, and finally back at him. "I, uh, it's the accident. I keep replaying it in my head. Every time I close my eyes, it's there. I hear it. I see it." She took a swallow and her voice cracked then lowered to a bare whisper. "And when I think what might have happened to Leah…"

Nick walked over to her and put his hands on her shoulders. "But nothing happened to Leah. You're going to be fine."

"My brain knows that." She closed her eyes for a second, then when she opened them again, granting him a soft look, something pierced through his gut. It was *something* that he didn't recognize. *Something* that was new and strange to him.

He touched her cheek and got lost in her eyes. He had a need to protect. To comfort. He brought his mouth close and brushed his lips to hers. The kiss was meant to reassure, to help her find some peace, but Nick didn't expect the sensations to rip through him. He didn't expect to want more. Sure, he'd once been attracted to Brooke. She'd been different than the other girls he'd been with in high school. There was substance to her, a depth that other girls didn't have at that age. She hadn't been a party girl. Maybe that's why Nick had been attracted to her. She was unique and special and Nick had realized that during the one night they'd spent together when he'd almost taken her virginity.

For years after, he'd wondered if he'd been really noble or scared that she was the one who could tie him down. And for years after he'd also imagined what it would have been like making love to her. Her first time. He'd wanted it to be with him, yet, he knew enough to back off. He'd done the right thing back then.

Her lips were warm and inviting. Devouring her heart-shaped mouth until she was swollen and puffy would be easy, but Nick pulled away. She gazed at him with a question in her eyes. He circled a lock of her long hair with his finger and tugged gently. "Just so you know, there aren't any strings attached to you staying here."

"I know," she said abruptly. "You're doing a good deed and you don't want an instant family. You're not interested, and buddy, neither am I."

She turned on her heel and walked off. He watched her stop to fight off a dizzy spell before climbing the stairs. He waited until she made it up to the second floor before looking away and smiling. Now he remembered why he liked her so much. She wasn't afraid to speak her mind and tell him off when she thought he needed it.

Three

Brooke lay in Nick's bed as fading sunshine spilled through the window. She'd never been one to sleep away the afternoon, but the doctor ordered rest and she would do anything to get out of the Carlino house as quickly as possible. So with Leah sleeping in her little playpen next to her and Nurse Jacobs in the adjoining room, Brooke punched the pillow and placed it under her head then forced her eyes closed.

But rest wasn't coming easy. Her little episode with Nick down by the pool played over in her mind. *Stupid, Brooke. You let him kiss you.*

Nick Carlino wasn't lacking in the kiss department. He knew what he was doing and always had. He was sexy down to the bone. Even with a dozen internal warnings screaming at her to back away from Nick, the second his lips touched hers, magic happened.

Foolishly, she'd gotten lost in his touch and taste, wanting more. More comfort. More reassurance. More magic. But Brooke wouldn't let the need inside her grow. She might have had a weak moment, but she'd be on guard now.

She took slow deep breaths, calming her nerves and letting all the tension ooze out of her body. The events of the past twenty-four hours had finally caught up to her. Her head ached less and less and sleep seemed possible now.

Nick left his group of friends at the window booth in the Cab Café, and headed her way. The minute Brooke spotted him approaching the counter her heart skipped some very necessary beats. Every time he came into the café with his friends she wanted to run and hide.

She wasn't one of them. The baseball jocks and their cheerleader girlfriends had their own exclusive club. Their friendliness ended with casual hellos. They wouldn't let her inside their circle, even if she wanted to be let in. She worked at the Cab Café and wore a purple and white uniform with an apron decorated with lavender grapes. She lived on the wrong side of town.

"Hi," Nick said, straddling the stool in front of her.

"Hi. What can I get you?" Brooke asked, as she passed him to set down coffee and a slice of peach pie for a customer.

"Would love a vanilla shake, but I'm in training. Just a lemonade." He smiled.

"You got it," Brooke said, trying not to stare at him. Nick Carlino had a set of dimples that made mush of her brains. "How's the team doing?"

"We won last night. I hit home run number twelve."

Brooke poured his lemonade and slid the glass over. "Is that a record?"

"Not yet, but I'm getting close. You should come to the games."

"I, uh, thanks. Maybe I will." Brooke had to work on the weekends. That's when they were the busiest. But Nick didn't know about things like that. He came from the privileged class and she doubted he knew anything about sacrifice or paying the bills.

"I hope so." He stared into her eyes so long, heat traveled up her neck.

Why did he care if she came to his baseball games? "I'll try."

He sipped his lemonade. "How'd you do on the trig test?"

"Got an A, but I sweated that one. You?"

"You beat me, Brooke." His blue eyes twinkled with mischief. "I don't like to lose."

It was official now. It wasn't just her brain melting—her entire body turned marshmallow-soft hearing him say her name. "Try studying. I hear it's a sure way to ace a test."

Nick chuckled and rose from the stool, taking the last sip of his lemonade. He laid down some money on the counter. He was a good tipper for a high school student. She moved on to her next customer at the counter and Nick walked away. When he reached the middle of the café, he turned back around and caught her eye one last time. "I've got a game tomorrow at three."

She nodded her acknowledgment just as the Victors' head cheerleader, Candy Rae Brenner, slipped her hand into Nick's and pulled him along, giving Brooke a dismissive look.

The dream startled her awake. But it wasn't a dream—it was a real memory. Brooke hadn't thought about that day in a long time. She didn't know why that particular scene entered her dreams, but it must have to do with the fact that she'd hit Nick's car and was sleeping in his bed.

She glanced at Leah beside her, all rosy cheeks and dark blonde curls wrapped into a sweet sleeping bundle. Leah made everything possible. She held her mama's heart in those tiny little hands.

Concentrate on her, Brooke. Forget about Nick. And the past.

But Brooke couldn't do it. The dream had been so real, so vivid that it triggered more memories of Nick. Those next few weeks entered her mind with stunning accuracy.

"You didn't come to the game." Nick caught up to her as she walked down the hall past the chemistry lab. School was out and she had a long walk home.

She glanced at him. Tremors of excitement erupted inside and she felt queasy from the turmoil stirring her stomach. Why was he walking with her? "I had to work. You know, some of us have to earn a living."

"Little Miss Attitude today, aren't you?"

"Me?" She pointed to her chest then realized her mistake. Nick's gaze followed the direction of her finger and he studied her chest. He raised his brows and stared some more. It figured she'd be wearing a tank top that revealed a modest amount of cleavage today.

She scurried past him but he caught up to her. "Hey, are you working after school?"

"Why?" she asked, curious what he wanted with her. "Need a study buddy for trig?"

Nick laughed. "Hell no. I'm getting a passing grade, that's good enough. As long as I keep my grades up, I'm on the team."

"And that's all that matters?"

Nick was a sure thing for the major league draft. The entire school rallied around him. He was the golden boy who earned okay grades and had a batting record that brought the scouts out in droves.

"For me, yeah. I'm not going to college. And I'm not working for my old man. It's baseball or nothing."

He had dreams, Brooke thought, and he'd probably attain them. He was after all, the golden boy. While Brooke faced community college and working to help her mother pay the bills, others would be off pursuing a life that would mean something important to them.

"So, are you working or not?"

"Later tonight I am," she answered.

"I'll drive you home."

She was ready to say no thanks, but then she looked into Nick's midnight blue eyes and hope swelled in her chest. Her heart wanted to say yes, but her brain got in the way. "Why?"

"Why what? Why do I want to drive you home?"

She furrowed her brows and nodded.

"Maybe I'm going that way." Then he leaned in closer and lowered his voice. "Or maybe I like you."

She laughed, thinking that would be the day, and looked away.

Nick moved in front of her so she had to face him. "Brooke?"

He said her name again in a tone that sounded sincere and…hopeful. It was the hopeful part that swept through her like a hurricane, obliterating all rational thought. She nodded and smiled. "Okay."

His world-class dimples emerged, stealing her breath. "C'mon, my car's in the parking lot."

Those last weeks in June before graduation were a combination of highs and lows. Whenever Nick didn't have practice after school, he'd drive her home and they'd sit on her front porch and talk about everything and anything. She'd learned a lot about his childhood, his baseball dreams and when he spoke of his mother, it was with fondness and love. Each day, Brooke had fallen more and more in love with him. It was a young girl's fascination, but the feelings she had for him were real. He'd never asked her on a date or tried to kiss her, which contradicted his reputation. He'd dated every popular girl on campus, Candy Rae being the latest in the string. Rumor had it that they'd broken up and Nick had alluded to it, but one thing he didn't talk about with Brooke was other girls.

She'd resigned herself to the fact that she was Nick's "friend" who lived on the other side of town. When prom came, Brooke had waited, but Nick never said a word, so she accepted a date with the busboy that worked with her at the Cab Café. She'd shown up in a dress she'd splurged on from her meager savings. Her mother, who had a great sense of style, had curled her hair and helped with makeup. When she spotted Nick at the dance with Candy Rae her heart sank. Though Nick had never promised her a thing, she felt hopeless and dejected, but was determined not to take it out on poor Billy Sizemore, her date. They'd danced and danced, and took pictures under the corny grapevine arbor inside the hall where the prom was held.

She came out of the ladies room and was instantly grabbed by the waist and pressed against the wall of a secluded corner by the bathroom. "Nick? What are you doing?"

"Just wanted to say hello."

"Hello," she droned without emotion.

The dimples of doom came out and Brooke had an uncanny urge to touch her fingertip to one.

"You look amazing." His gaze swept over her hair, her dress, her body and then he looked deep into her eyes. "You have incredible eyes. It's the first thing I noticed about you."

Nick was deadly handsome and so near, she could

hardly breathe. What she couldn't figure out was why he was torturing her.

"I didn't want to bring Candy Rae here," he confessed. "The fact is, she made me promise months ago."

"And you don't break your promises?"

"Try not to. Her mother called my father last week to make sure I'd follow through. He put the old Italian guilt on me."

"Why are you telling me this?"

He looked at her quizzically. "You don't know?"

She shook her head.

He reached out to touch her hair, his gaze flowing over her face. A long moment passed and then he bent his head and kissed her.

Brooke couldn't believe this was happening. His lips were just like she imagined, amazingly warm and giving, a prelude and a promise of more to come. Brooke had waited so long for this, for him, that at first she just remained there enjoying the sensations rippling through her, frozen like an ice sculpture and melting a little at a time.

He wrapped his arms around her and she found herself immersed in Nick Carlino, his touch, his scent, his body pressed to hers. And she was through holding back. She returned his kiss with everything she had inside. He kissed her again, his mouth more demanding now, and a wild sort of frenzy built. Lust combined with the love she held in her heart for him and everything else faded from her mind. He parted her lips and drove his tongue into her mouth. Sensations whirled and she let out tiny gasps as he devoured her, his desire overwhelming.

Overhead, an announcement rang out calling for the last dance.

"I've got to go," he said with a low rasp. He backed away from her but the regret in his eyes bolstered her spirit.

Things had gotten out of control. Wonderfully so and she knew that when she went to sleep that night, her dreams would be of Nick.

Nurse Jacobs entered her room to take her blood pressure and temperature. Brooke waited patiently, sitting upright on the bed, while the older, sweet-faced woman removed the cuff and took the digital thermometer out of her mouth.

"All looks good, Mrs. Keating. Your blood pressure is normal and so is your temperature. How about the dizzy spells?"

She'd told the nurse once already not to call her Mrs. Keating. She hated the reminder of her marriage. "It's Brooke, remember? And I had a slight dizzy spell earlier, but nothing for a few hours."

The nurse looked pleased. "The rest is doing you good. Now, if I could get you to eat something. Mr. Carlino said that dinner would be ready at six. Are you up to going downstairs or shall I bring food up to you?"

"Oh, no. That's not necessary. We'll go down."

Leah began to stir and she knew her baby had enough of napping. She'd want some stimulation and learning about these new surroundings would satisfy her curiosity. Brooke would take her outside later to get some air as well.

"She's a good baby and a good sleeper." Nurse Jacobs smiled at Leah. "My children weren't good sleepers. I tried everything, but they were determined to keep their mom up most of the night. But they were good kids after that. Didn't give me a wink of trouble as teenagers."

"I guess you can't ask for more than that," Brooke said, suddenly curious about the nurse. "Are they grown now?"

"My son is finishing up college at Berkeley. My daughter,

she's the older one, is married and I'm hoping she'll make me a grandmother one day."

Brooke thought about her own mother. She'd had a tough life and was finally married again and living in Hawaii with her new husband, a widower and former naval officer with a kind heart who thought the sun rose and set on her mother's shoulders. Brooke was glad of it and though they missed each other, she knew her mother would spend some extended visits with them once Brooke and Leah settled into their new home.

"My mom is really crazy about Leah," Brooke said. "We saw her last month and—"

Leah fussed, letting out a complaining cry. Brooke stood up to go to her, but the room spun instantly and she reached out for the bed to steady herself. She closed her eyes until the feeling passed.

Nurse Jacobs was beside her quickly and braced her around the waist. "You stood up too fast," she said softly. "Move slow and make each step deliberate. How's your head now?"

Brooke glanced at her. Everything began to clear. "Better."

"Let me get Leah for you. Have a seat and I'll diaper her and bring her to you so you can nurse her."

Brooke did as she was told. The sooner she recovered, the better. She didn't want to be beholden to Nick for anything more. She already owed him for the damages to his car and for room and board, not to mention for the private nurse he'd hired to care for her. Brooke vowed to pay him back once her establishment started making money.

An hour later, Brooke had showered, changed her clothes, put a little blush on her pale cheeks and felt human again. She dressed Leah in a sundress and sandals that matched her own—a gift from Grandma "for her two girls," her mother had written on the gift card. Thankfully, her mom was provided for now and could spend money without pinching pennies and she'd lavished so many wonderful things on Leah.

Brooke smiled.

"That smile looks good on you. Feeling better?"

"Much. I'm ready to go down for dinner."

"I'll take Leah, if you can manage the stairs."

"I'll help Brooke down," Nick said, standing in the opened doorway and nodding at the nurse. He wore a black Polo shirt that displayed lean muscles and tanned olive skin. His pants were beige, expensive and fit his frame perfectly.

"I can manage."

Nurse Jacobs touched her arm. "Let him help you, Brooke. Just in case."

Brooke hesitated, but now wasn't the time to be obstinate. "Well, okay."

Nick waited until they reached the top of the staircase before putting his arm around her waist. She felt the gentle pressure of his touch all the way down to her toes. If nurse Jacobs only knew what a dizzying effect Nick had on her, she wouldn't have encouraged this.

"I'm glad you decided to come down for dinner. I thought you were still annoyed at me from before."

"I'm not in a position to be annoyed. You're being very... gracious."

"So out of character for me, right?"

"No comment," Brooke said, but she smiled and Nick didn't seem to take offense.

Once they made it down the stairs, Nick led them to the terrace where a table was set under a slatted patio roof held up by stone columns. "We're between cooks right now, so I ordered in. You'd end up back in the hospital if I tried my hand at cooking."

"That's fine, thank you," she said, then reached for Leah. "Come here, pretty baby." She kissed Leah's cheek the minute Nurse Jacobs handed her over. She settled Leah onto her lap. The baby was still groggy from her long nap.

The housekeeper, Carlotta, made a big fuss over Leah, offering to hold her while Brooke ate her meal, but she kindly refused. She still hadn't gotten over the accident and what could have happened. She wanted Leah near and she'd eaten this way, with Leah on her lap, dozens of times. It was a ritual that she'd soon have to break. Leah was growing in leaps and bounds and would need a high chair soon.

Carlotta made sure they were served and wanted for nothing. Brooke was amazed at how hungry she was, satisfying her growling pangs with shrimp salad, pasta primavera and creamy pesto chicken. She ate with gusto as Nick and her nurse conversed about growing up in Napa. Nick was a charmer and by the end of the meal, her middle-aged nurse was surely smitten. Every so often, Nick would catch Brooke's eye and they'd exchange a glance. Heat traveled through her body even as she pretended not to notice his effect on her.

Carlotta served a decadent Italian dessert catered from a restaurant Nick's family owned. The oozing lava cake exploded with melted chocolate the minute Brooke touched her fork to the center. Leah grabbed at her fork with her chubby grasp and a spray of liquid chocolate splattered onto Brooke's chest. The baby giggled and swiped at the confection again, tipping it over.

"Leah!" Brooke shook her head as she glanced at her freshly stained white blouse and the puddle of chocolate her child made on the table.

Carlotta and her nurse rushed into the kitchen to repair the damage, leaving Brooke alone at the table with Nick.

"Look what you've done to Mommy." Leah giggled again and Brooke had to smile, unable to feel any anger at the situation. Though she imagined she looked a total mess now. "You're getting me all chocolately and—"

"Delicious," Nick said softly, gazing into her eyes. He slipped a forkful of dessert into his mouth, but his eyes remained on her.

She didn't know how to react. Was he coming on to her? Any embarrassment she might have felt dissolved just seeing the spark of intensity in Nick's eyes. Did she want his flirting, even just for her own deflated ego?

"Here, Carlotta gave me this." Nurse Jacobs returned and handed her a wet dishcloth. "It might not stain if you get to it quickly."

"Oh, I'll probably just take it off upstairs and work on it," she said, holding Leah on her lap with one hand while dabbing at the splashes of chocolate with the other hand.

Carlotta walked onto the patio with a pained expression. "Nick, you have a visitor."

Nick glanced up as a sultry dark-haired woman breezed onto the patio.

"Hi, Nicky."

"Rachel." Nick got out of his seat.

The woman was stunning, even if she was a bit older than Nick. Looking proprietary, she placed her hand on his shoulder and lifted up on her toes to kiss him.

Brooke looked away rather than intrude on an intimate moment. She wondered what Rachel would say if she knew Nick had kissed her just hours ago, on this very same terrace.

"Who are your friends?" the woman inquired, staring at Nick.

He made the introductions without qualms. Rachel followed the direction of Nick's gaze and swept a quick glance at Brooke and the baby, noting her stained blouse without missing a beat.

Brooke had learned not to give in to humiliation anymore. She lifted her chin and greeted Nick's girlfriend with a poise that could win her an Oscar. "It's nice to meet you, Rachel."

"Rachel owns A Rock and A Hard Place," Nick offered.

Brooke furrowed her brow. "I don't remember it."

"It's a bar and nightclub," Rachel explained. "I opened it about three years ago and I guess you could say it's my baby." Rachel looked at Leah. "Until the real thing comes along, that is." She glanced at Nick, who held an unreadable expression, then turned her attention to Leah. "She's adorable."

"Thank you. She's quite a mess at the moment. Both of us are. I should probably clean us both up."

When Brooke rose from the table, Nurse Jacobs stepped up and reached for Leah. "I'll take her for you."

"Thank you," Brooke said, her glance darting from Rachel to Nick. "I'll leave you two alone. Have a nice evening."

Nick met her eyes. "Think you can make it upstairs okay?"

Brooke nodded. "I'm feeling better. Thanks for dinner." She waved her hand over her blemished blouse. "For as much as I managed to get into my mouth, it was *delicious*."

Nick's eyes went wide, then he chuckled and Brooke walked off feeling his gaze on her.

She heard Rachel question him with one word. *"Upstairs?"*

And she scurried a bit faster into the house.

* * *

Nick leaned against the railing that overlooked the valley below, his beer held between two fingers as he took a swig. He'd sipped champagne with the monks in France and enjoyed the best wines in all of Europe, not to mention imbibing from the best-ranked vintages in the family wine cellar, but tonight he needed good all-American beer.

His father would cringe seeing the cases of beer Nick had stocked in the house. Carlinos didn't drink beer. Carlinos were winemakers. His father never came to grips with the fact that none of his sons wanted to be winemakers. They had separate interests, which were, of course, of no concern to the man who'd fathered them. Once Nick's mother died, the boys were treated to Santo Carlino's constant demands on how they should live their lives.

Tony and Joe had escaped relatively unscathed, but Nick hadn't been so lucky. His father had managed to ruin Nick's career, before it had even started.

"I'm pregnant, Nick," Candy Rae cried into the phone right before his debut minor league baseball game. *"I'm scared and I need you. Come home."*

Nick couldn't come home. He'd been drafted by the Chicago White Sox. He was making his first start on the triple AAA squad on the Charlotte Knights and he needed to perform. He needed to make his mark and prove himself.

While he assured Candy Rae he'd come home and deal with the situation as soon as he could, she wouldn't let up. She'd called him every day for weeks and the calls sapped his concentration on the ball field, so much so that he stopped taking her calls. Next thing he knew, Candy Rae showed up at the ballpark and pleaded with him in person to come home. She was six months pregnant and the evidence of his child growing inside her couldn't be missed. He didn't love Candy Rae, but he'd make sure his child wanted for nothing. He'd have a part in raising the baby but that wasn't good enough for her. She wanted Nick home. She wanted marriage and the white picket fence fairy tale. Candy Rae was spoiled and stubborn and she put up a huge fuss, crying, screaming and stomping her feet. They argued, Nick not giving in to her tantrum and an hour later Nick walked onto the baseball field.

Distracted and pissed off, he'd collided with his teammate trying to make a catch in the outfield. He'd dislocated his shoulder, requiring surgery and a long recovery time.

"Should've been a piece of cake," Nick muttered, sipping his ice-cold beer in the warm Napa night, thinking about that catch *and* the recovery.

The house on the hill was quiet. Only a few stars lit the sky and it was the remote silence surrounding him that brought back his desolation and disappointment. His life could have been so different.

He'd found out late that summer that Candy Rae's baby wasn't his but he'd also found out that his father had put her up to the deception. They'd schemed together to get what they wanted and both wanted the same thing, Nick to come home to Napa. Candy Rae claimed she loved him and Santo wanted a son he could groom to take over the family business.

Nick was released from his minor league contract after that injury and to this day, he'd bet his life his father had his hands in that. Santo was an unscrupulous manipulator. He'd had a reputation for being a ruthless businessman and his business always came first with him.

Nick never forgave him for that…for messing with his dream.

After that fiasco, he'd moved out of the country for many years, becoming the foreign liaison for Carlino Wines in European markets. This was all he could stomach to do, working for the family business—needing time and distance away from Santo. Nick managed other interests overseas, making sound real estate investments. He'd become wealthy in his own right before long.

Nick heard footsteps on the grounds and turned to find Brooke coming out of the house, barefoot, wearing a silky robe. Her long blond hair spilled onto her shoulders. He watched her take a few steps onto the terrace.

She hadn't seen him yet—he was in the shadows—and that was fine with him. He could look at her without her defenses going up. Cascading terrace lamps lit her in a halo of light. Her movements graceful, she stepped farther out onto the terrace, taking in deep breaths of air. She looked troubled, as if searching for peace.

When she spotted him, she jumped back. "Oh, sorry," she whispered. "I didn't think anyone would be out here this late."

"Neither did I. Couldn't sleep?"

"Not tired. I think I got too much rest this afternoon. Looks like you're enjoying the peace. I'll just go back upstairs." She turned and took a step.

"Don't go." Nick cursed under his breath. He was in a dangerous mood and it would be better for her to go inside.

She stopped but didn't turn to face him. "I should go up."

Nick pushed off from the railing and strode over until he was behind her and near enough to whisper in her ear. "You should. But I don't want you to."

Nick put his arms around her waist and brought her close. He'd always liked Brooke. She was unique and fresh with a clever sense of humor. She could make him laugh and he admired her gutsy attitude, while being beautiful and sexy at the same time. She was the girl that got away and she'd remain so, but right now, he wanted her company. And maybe a little bit more.

He felt her trembling in his arms. "What happened to Rachel?"

"She wanted something I can't give her."

Brooke hesitated, then finally whispered quietly, "What's that?"

"All of me."

Nick reached up and took Brooke's hair in his hand. He moved soft strands off her neck and kissed her there. Goose bumps erupted on her nape and Nick drew her closer to whisper, "And you want none of me. Are you holding a grudge?"

"Not a grudge. I told you before."

"Then what, Brooke?"

She turned around to face him. He was hit with an immediate jolt when she stared at him with those beyond-beautiful eyes. "Why does it matter?"

"You were important to me. We were friends once."

Brooke's mouth gaped open then she hauled off and shoved at his chest. Startled by her sudden move, he struggled to keep his balance.

"You are so dense!" Brooke seemed to shout, though it came out in a loud whisper.

Nick looked at her and the absurdity of the conversation struck his funny bone. He laughed. "What the hell are you talking about?"

"You see, you don't even know!"

"So why don't you tell me?" Judging by the look on her face, maybe he didn't want to know.

"You used the 'F' word."

"I did not," he said adamantly and then it dawned on him. He arched a brow. "Oh, okay. So I said we were friends."

Brooke turned to leave. 'I'm not having this conversation," she said as she stepped into the house.

Damn it. The woman was always walking away. He marched after her. "Sit down, Brooke."

She stopped in his living room and glared at him. "Is that an order?"

Nick was through being amused. Why he cared to clear the air with her was beyond him. Maybe it was the mood he was in. Maybe it was hearing Rachel accuse him of using her that got to him tonight. Maybe it was because she'd also accused him of not having a heart. Or maybe it's because he thought he'd done the right thing for once in his life and Brooke was punishing him for it.

He shouldn't give a damn.

But he did.

"Hell, Brooke. Cut me some slack. Talk to me."

Brooke glanced at the sofa and twisted her lips. "I could claim fatigue. I think I feel a dizzy spell coming on."

"Sit," he said, keeping his tone light.

She sat down on the sofa and he took the seat across from her. A glass and wrought-iron coffee table separated them. The room was dark but for the dim lamp light from the terrace filtering inside.

Nick waited.

Then Brooke began. "You were the last person on earth I ever wanted to see again."

"I know that. Now tell me why."

Four

Brooke's memories came rushing back of that one night that had changed her life forever. It wasn't what Nick had done but what he hadn't done that had devastated her young heart.

The pounding on the door startled Brooke out of a sound sleep. She raced down the hallway in her nightie, certain that something was wrong. Her mother was visiting her best friend in San Francisco for the weekend and Brooke feared something terrible had happened to her. Why else would someone be pounding on her door after ten o'clock at night?

She hesitated behind the door, until she heard his voice. "It's me, Brooke. It's Nick. C'mon. Open up." She heard the excitement in his voice and immediately yanked the door open.

He stood in the moonlight, grinning from ear to ear and she came alive right then, as if she'd been an empty shell until Nick appeared to breathe new life into her. She smiled instantly, his obvious joy contagious. "Nick? What is it?"

He lifted her off her feet and twirled her around and around in dizzying circles. "I did it. I did it. I'm going to the major leagues. I got drafted by the White Sox in the fifth round."

Before she had time to react, he set her down, cupped her face in his hands and kissed her with such intensity she thought she was still floating above ground. When he broke off the kiss, the hungry look in his blue eyes held her captivated. "Nick, that's great. It's what you want."

"I know. I know. I'm going to Charlotte to play for the Knights. It's Triple A ball, but if I play to my potential, Coach thinks it won't take long to make it to the majors."

"Oh, Nick. You'll get there. If you want it bad enough, you'll get there."

Without his knowledge, she'd gone to a play-off game and watched him play once. He'd been the star of the team. Everyone cheered for Nick when he stepped up to the plate. He'd hit three home runs in that weekend series and the team had gone on to win the championship.

"I came right over to tell you. I wanted you to know. I wanted to share this with you first."

He'd come to her, before telling his friends? Warmth rushed through her body and when he reached for her again and kissed her, Brooke's world turned upside down.

"I want you, Brooke," he whispered urgently, bracing her waist and tugging her close. Her legs rubbed against his jeans. "I've always wanted you."

He lavished kisses on her forehead, her eyes, her nose, her cheeks and then devoured her mouth in another long, fiery crazed kiss that lit her body on fire. "My mom's out of town," she whispered and Nick wasted no time.

"Where's your room?"

Brooke led him there and stood by the bed. He smiled and in one smooth move, he lifted her nightie and filled his hands with her breasts. The exquisite feel of his palms on her sent a hot thrill through her body. Deft fingers stroked her nipples and she ached for more. When he put his mouth on her, she squeezed her eyes shut from the exquisite, sweet torture.

Nick had her naked on the bed in seconds, then he removed his shirt and joined her. She was glad she'd waited, glad to have her first time be with Nick, the boy who'd been out of her reach for so long. Now, he was here, wanting her.

She loved him with a fierceness that stunned her. His touch sent her spiraling out of control. He kissed her a dozen times, driving her insane with his tongue, as he caressed every inch of her body.

Inexperienced and awkward, Brooke didn't know what to do. What would he expect from her? Should she be touching him back?

"This is a good night…being with you," he whispered, nibbling on her throat. His softly spoken words abolished her insecurities.

His hand traveled lower, his fingers seeking her warmth, and electric shocks powered through her body. She stiffened from the new sensation. She'd never felt anything like it, the intimacy of the act, the way he knew how to find her most sensitive spot and stroke her until she was breathless and mindless.

The sensation built and built and she arched and moaned until only little cries of ecstasy escaped her lips. Wave after wave of release shattered her and Nick stroked her harder, faster, drawing out her orgasm, his eyes dark and filled with desire. He murmured soft words but she didn't hear him, didn't recognize what he was asking until she felt the last tiny wave leave her.

"Are you protected?" he asked again.

And she looked at him and shook her head. "I don't have, I mean I don't—"

He stood up and reached into his pocket, then something stopped him. She'd never forget the look on his face, the way he studied her as she lay naked on the bed.

"Nick?" Dread beat against her chest and her stomach coiled.

He stared at her and blinked. His gaze roved over her again and this time she truly felt naked and strangely alone. Then the unthinkable happened. Nick shook his head, closing his eyes to her and taking deep breaths. "I can't do this, Brooke. I'm gonna have to leave."

"Nick?" Panicked, Brooke lifted up to reach for him.

To her horror, he backed away, as if repulsed by her touch. "I gotta go, Brooke. I can't. I'm sorry."

Mortified, Brooke watched him grab his shirt and walk out of her bedroom.

"Brooke?" Nick asked, glancing at her intently.

Sudden anger strangled the words she wanted to say to him. She wanted to blast him with full guns and then walk out of his house and forget she ever laid eyes on him again. But she bit back her remarks and calmed down to a rational level. "You hurt me, Nick. That night. The night you got drafted."

His sharp breath was audible. "None of that was supposed to happen."

That's all he had to say? He'd broken her heart and left her shattered, wishing that she'd been enough for him. The girl from the right side of town. The girl he'd want to take out on a date and introduce to his family, the girl who didn't work at the local diner and sewed her own clothes.

She'd dared to hope, but that hope had been crushed.

She wasn't even good enough to have a one-night fling with. He'd rejected her and left her lying there, exposed and vulnerable and humiliated.

"How do you think I felt when you walked out on me?"

"You should have been relieved," Nick said in earnest, and she wanted to shove him in the chest again.

"Relieved? How can you say that? You…you led me on. You came to my house that night with one thing on your mind."

"Things shouldn't have gone that far, Brooke. I realized that and I walked out before we made a mistake."

"A mistake?" Inwardly she cringed. Now she was a *mistake*. This conversation was going from bad to worse and Brooke wanted to scream out in frustration.

Nick leaned forward, bracing the back of his elbows on his knees. "You were special to me, Brooke and—"

"I was your good buddy," she spit out.

"No, you were the girl I wanted the most and the one I couldn't let myself have."

Brooke shook her head. "I don't get it. Your memory must be failing you. Age does that to a person. You must be old before your time."

"You see," Nick said with a grin. "You're clever and feisty and pretty. Listen, I may have had a reputation back then—"

"Similar to the one you have now," she butted in.

"R-right. But I didn't want to lump you in with the other girls I dated."

"You never *dated* me. Are you going to tell me that's because I was so special?"

"I was afraid of you."

"What?" Brooke sat back in her seat, thunderstruck. Nothing he said was sinking in, but this, *this* was too ridiculous to even consider. "Big, bad Brooke."

"Sweet, special, smart Brooke," he said.

Her anger rose. His compliments meant nothing to her. "Stop! Just stop, Nick," she rushed out. "Why don't you just admit the truth! I didn't measure up to the other girls in your string. You got me naked and decided you could do better. Isn't that what really happened? I was inexperienced and I don't know, maybe I wasn't doing the right things and you—"

"Let me get this straight," he said, between clenched teeth. "You're angry because we didn't screw like rabbits all night long? Here I was trying to be noble, to do the right thing, and you're upset because I didn't take your virginity?"

"I cared about you," she said, raising her voice. "I wanted it to be with you."

"And I didn't want to use you. Damn it, the one time I do the right thing I get kicked in the ass. Listen, Brooke. I wasn't sticking around. At that time, my life, my future was baseball. I was leaving the next week for the minor leagues. And yeah, you scared me, because of all the girls I'd been with you were the one girl who could tie me down. The one girl I'd miss when I took off. It wouldn't have worked. I didn't want to hurt you. I never meant to."

"But you did," she said quietly. "You devastated me, Nick. I never heard from you again. Ever."

I was deeply in love with you.

She opened up to him, finally confessing what she'd held back all these years, "Just think of all the worst things you think about yourself, your secret innermost thoughts that nag at you day after day, that you're nothing, not pretty enough, not smart enough, not wealthy enough, not *anything* and to have those very thoughts confirmed by the one person in the world who can change your opinion. You leaving me there that night confirmed the worst about myself."

Nick came around the coffee table to sit beside her. From the dim lights, she could see into his eyes, the sorrow there and the apology. He didn't try to touch her, but those eyes penetrating hers were like the tightest embrace. "I'm sorry. I thought I did the right thing for you. I've never been one to hold back when I wanted something, but what I did that night, it was for you. I wanted you, Brooke. But it wouldn't have been fair to you."

Brooke had clung to her perceptions about Nick for so long it was hard to let them go. She wanted to believe him and release the bitter feelings that had only dragged her down these past years. She wanted to be done with it. She had a future to look forward to now with Leah. Finally she resigned herself to accept Nick's claim as the truth as he saw it. "Okay, Nick."

It still didn't make up for the months of anguish she'd experienced or for the heartache of loving someone like Nick, but she realized it was finally time to move on.

"Okay?" Nick said. "We've cleared the air?"

She nodded. "Yes."

And they sat in silence for a long while, just absorbing the conversation.

"I think I'm well enough to leave tomorrow," Brooke said finally. "I've got a new life waiting for me." She rose from the sofa. "I should go."

Nick nodded, but his response left room for doubt. "We'll see."

Brooke dressed Leah in a blue-and-white-polka-dotted short set with a ruffled collar and bloomers. She combed her hair and hummed the *Sesame Street* song, laughing as Leah's stubborn curls popped right back up the minute she put the brush down. The morning seemed filled with promise. She'd had a lot to absorb from her encounter with Nick last night and she'd slept on it, waking this morning with a better attitude and ready to put the past behind her.

"It's gonna be a good day, baby girl," she said, lifting Leah up and twirling her around. A wave of light-headedness hit her and Brooke stopped and let it pass, clutching her child tight. "Your mommy is pushing her luck," she whispered.

Nurse Jacobs entered the room, dressed and ready to take over. "Time to take your vitals," she said to Brooke.

Brooke complied, having her blood pressure and temperature taken. When the nurse finished her exam, she gave her a reassuring smile. "You look well-rested."

"I'm feeling much better today."

"You got dizzy just a second ago."

Brooke didn't think she'd seen that. "Stupid of me to spin Leah around. I won't do that again. We're going down for breakfast."

"Okay, I'll hold Leah on the way downstairs."

"Actually, I'd like to hold her."

Nurse Jacobs narrowed her eyes and debated until Brooke added, "You'll be right by my side. We'll go down together."

Once it was all settled, they headed to the kitchen. They heard cupboards being opened and slammed shut and curses being muttered by Nick in hushed tones. The odor of burnt toast filled the air. Brooke walked in with Leah in her arms, took one look at the kitchen in disarray with greasy frying pans on the stovetop, blackened bread in the toaster and Nick, dressed in a pair of jeans and a white T-shirt that hugged his male frame, looking frustrated and out of sorts.

Brooke immediately grinned. "I didn't feel the tornado this morning. Did you, Leah?"

The baby looked at her quizzically.

Nick cast Brooke a quick glance. "Carlotta's got the morning off, not that she cooks anyway, but at least she can boil water and make toast. Looks like I can do neither."

Brooke took in the state-of-the-art appliances and fully functional workstation. "It's a great kitchen. You don't have a cook?"

"Not since my father passed away. The cook retired and we've managed without her up until now. Tony's gone and Joe spends his time at the office or with his fiancée. Which leaves me. I've been fending for myself, not very well I might add, interviewing a little, but no one's worked out." He picked up the phone. "I'll call for delivery. What would you ladies like for breakfast?"

Brooke shook her head. "Jeez, that bump on my head didn't obliterate my cooking skills. I'll fix breakfast. It's the least I can do. I make a mean omelet. Let me at this kitchen and I'll have breakfast on the table in half an hour." Nick put the phone down slowly and Brooke took over. "Here, hold Leah a minute while I raid your refrigerator."

She put Leah in Nick's arms and her daughter snuggled in looking comfortable, while Nick looked anything but. He tried to hand her off to Nurse Jacobs and the wily nurse stepped back and shook her head. "*Brooke* is my patient." She winked at Brooke. Nick sat down at the kitchen table with a twist of his lips and Leah latched onto his shirt.

Brooke opened his double stainless steel refrigerator and

began taking out ingredients. "It's well stocked, which is good news." She immersed herself in her task, enjoying the process. She quickly whipped together three of the lightest, fluffiest omelets she'd ever made, pan-fried potatoes and a fresh fruit salad. Coffee brewed in the pot and while she cooked, Nurse Jacobs set the table.

"How's Leah doing over there?" Brooke asked. She'd been keeping an eye on the two of them.

"Is she always this fidgety?" Nick asked as Leah tried to crawl her way up his chest. She pulled at his shirt and brought her little hand up to swipe at his chin. He set her back down onto his lap. "I think I liked her better when she was sleeping."

Brooke smiled. "She's an absolute *angel*...when she's sleeping. Okay, all set. I'll dish it up. I hope you like lots of veggies and avocado."

There was still tension between them, but she wouldn't have to deal with it too much longer because Brooke was leaving today. She was eager and excited at the prospect of starting her own business.

She served the meal and silence ensued. With Leah on her lap, she dug into the omelet and tasted. Not bad. Then she glanced at Nick's plate to find he'd gobbled up the omelet already and was working on the potatoes. "Want another?" she asked.

"In a heartbeat. Finish yours first. I'll work on what's left on my plate."

A few minutes later, Brooke started cooking Nick's second omelet and Nurse Jacobs took Leah outside for a little stroll.

Nick leaned over the black granite counter, elbows folded, watching her put the bell peppers, onions, bits of ham and grated cheese onto the egg mix and top it off with avocado. "So we're good, about last night. No hard feelings?"

Brooke met his gaze, waiting for the hurt, anger and bitterness to emerge. When it didn't appear, her heart lifted. She and Nick came from different worlds. They were never destined to be together and maybe…just maybe she might believe that he had spared her that night. Yet her initial thoughts from her high school days hadn't changed. He was way out of her league. If she were looking for a man, he wouldn't be last on her list—he wouldn't be *on* it at all. He wasn't a man to stick around. Nick was a player and Brooke had already played the game and lost. And while that might be okay for her, it wasn't all right for Leah. Her daughter's needs always had to come first.

"No hard feelings. But we have to talk about something else. Have you heard back from your mechanic?"

"I have."

"And? What's the bad news?"

He frowned. "Your car might live."

"That's not bad news! That's great."

She flipped the omelet over and lifted it with a spatula then grabbed Nick's plate from the table. "I was hoping it wasn't totaled." She loaded the omelet onto the dish and set it in front of him.

He took his fork and began eating. "How do you do it? This is better than the last one and that one was pretty damn good."

"I'm amazing. I can make an omelet."

Nick scoffed. "You're a good cook, Brooke. Admit it."

"I do okay. So how much is it gonna cost for the repairs?"

"It's taken care of."

She blinked and stood completely still. "No, Nick. It's not. Both of our cars were damaged. I owe somebody, something. I plan to pay. Do you have an estimate?"

"I do."

"Well, where is it? Show it to me," she ordered.

Nick scratched his head and stared at her. She glared back and held her ground. He reached into his pocket and pulled out two pieces of paper from Napa Auto Body Works. Unfolding the papers, he laid them onto the counter and turned them her way.

"Thirteen thousand dollars for your car! You can practically buy a new car for that!" Of course she'd had to collide into *Nick* and the *most* expensive car on the planet.

"My insurance will cover most of it."

Relieved about that, Brooke peered at her estimate. "Forty-eight hundred dollars." She breathed a heavy sigh. That would cut heavily into the money she had saved to start her business, not to mention fixing up the place. The broken interior door would have to wait, and so would the painters and new linens she'd need for the beds. And fixing the bathrooms. Still, she couldn't make *any* repairs without her car. She needed wheels. "When can I have my car back?"

"Maybe you should get another car. Randy said it was borderline. He could fix your car but it's almost not worth it."

"I can't do that. I can't afford a newer car."

Annoyed that Nick would think it just that easy for her to buy a car, she turned away, working out her frustration by scrubbing the frying pan in the sink.

A long minute stretched out in silence.

"Brooke, turn around." Nick was sure bossy this morning. She turned. "Listen, I have a proposition for you. I've got a 2006 Lexus just sitting in the garage waiting to be driven. The insurance is paid up on it for the rest of the year. It's yours if you want it."

She laughed at the thought, shaking her head. "Yeah, you'll just give me a car."

"Not give. You'll work it off."

"Work it off?" Her smile faded instantly. She closed her eyes to small slits. "I feel the need to slap you coming on."

"Cooking," he explained.

"Cooking?"

"You need a car. I need a cook. Correct that, I desperately need a cook. Carlotta's been a pain about who she'll let into the house. The last cook I tried to hire had Carlotta threatening to quit, but she'll jump for joy at having you here."

She immediately began shaking her head. "No, it wouldn't work. I've got a job. I'm going to be spending all my time at my aunt's place. My place now."

"You said yourself, it's in bad shape. You can stay here while you work on your place." The idea seemed to take hold, snowballing as Nick became more adamant. "I'd only need you for breakfast and dinner. You'd have all day to work at the house."

"I'm not staying here."

"You shouldn't have made me that omelet, Brooke. My stomach's involved now. You need the car. I'm tired of eating restaurant food. It'll work out for both of us. Think about it."

She didn't' want to think about it. She didn't, but his offer was too good not to at least give it some thought. "How long before I earned the car?"

"For as long as you need to get your place up and running. A couple of months?"

"That's very generous of you, but I can't—"

"Your car doesn't have air bags," he pointed out none too gently. "You'd be foolish to fix that car."

She squeezed her eyes shut, reminded of what might have happened. The accident could have been far worse.

"Think of Leah," he added without missing a beat.

She was thinking of Leah, constantly. And harrowing thoughts of that accident struck her with fear. She'd actually lost consciousness when they'd collided. What if she hadn't run into someone she'd known? What would have happened to Leah then? She didn't want to take Nick's offer. But Leah's safety came first. She remembered what the flight attendants always said in their little welcome aboard speech about putting an oxygen mask on yourself first, before putting one on for your child. The bottom line, in order to care for your child, you must take care of yourself.

Brooke craved independence and wanted to be indebted to no one. Living under Nick Carlino's roof wouldn't be an option if she were thinking only about herself. But of course, Nick had the upper hand and was on the right side of the argument. Small wonder—he negotiated for Carlino Wines, and knew when to finesse and when to land the crushing blow. This time, he'd used Leah as his weapon and Brooke was defeated.

"That's low, Nick. You know I always have Leah's welfare at heart. What's in it for you?"

"I'm selfish enough to want to eat good meals. And keep the housekeeper from walking out. Do we have a deal?"

Brooke's mouth turned down as she accepted. "Hand over the keys and tell me what you want for dinner."

The dimples of doom came out when he smiled and Brooke didn't find them attractive at all.

Not even a little bit.

"You're joking, right? You've got Brooke Hamilton *living* with you now? I thought it was only temporary." Joe glanced at Tony as they sat at their monthly meeting at the Carlino offices in downtown Napa. His two brothers shook their heads in disapproval. "You're good, little brother," Joe said, "but I didn't know how good. You met her what, twenty-four hours ago?"

Normally, Nick didn't let his brothers get to him, but right now he wasn't in the mood for their wisecracking. He spoke through tight lips. "It was two days ago. And more like she met with the front end of my Ferrari. She's working for me, to pay off her debt." Hell, he made her sound like an indentured servant. With a brisk wave of the hand, he added, "It's complicated."

Tony's laughter filled the air. "Complicated as in a honey blonde with pretty blue eyes."

"You liked her back in high school," Joe said. "You know what they say about the one that got away."

"She's got a baby," Nick said in his defense. "Or are you forgetting about the kid?"

"You think that's gonna stop you?" Tony looked skeptical.

"Hell yeah." Nick wasn't father material. He'd learned from the master. He had enough of his old man in him to know he wouldn't make a good daddy. The blood ties ran thick. He never planned on having children, thus saving some poor child his ruthless tendencies.

"We think not," Tony said glibly, leaning back in his chair and stretching out. He darted a glance at Joe.

"Then, you think wrong," Nick said, ready to change the subject.

After Candy Rae's deception, Nick had lost faith in the opposite sex. Not that he didn't love women, but he wouldn't be foolish enough to place his trust in a female again. He'd lost out on his dream because of Candy Rae's lies and his father's self-serving manipulations. He'd been crushed and trampled on like the precious grapes that his father had loved so much. For that, he hated what he did for a living, feeling his father had won. Nick spent most of his time in Europe, away from the place that caused him such heartache. He'd made enough smart financial investments to break loose of his father's ties forever and was about to do so, but then Santo up and died. Nick came home because his brothers needed him. He was here because of them even though they were a pain in his rear end. Nick liked things simple and getting too involved with Brooke and her bundle of trouble would only complicate his life.

"Want to put money on it?" Tony said, baiting him.

"Damn right," Nick said. "A betting man always likes to take money from suckers. Name your price."

Joe sat straight up in his seat and Nick saw his brother do mental calculations. "What if it's not for cash? What if we wager something more important?"

"Like what?" Nick furrowed his brows.

"Like if you fall for her, you take over the company."

Nick fell back against his seat in shock.

"I like it," Tony said. "The nameplate on the door will read, Nick Carlino, CEO."

"Don't go counting your chickens. I haven't agreed to this yet. Seems this is a little lopsided. What do I get if I win?"

Joe didn't hesitate to answer. "Easy, if you win and you don't fall hard for that gorgeous woman and her little girl, you're completely off the hook. You'll get your fair share of the empire but you won't have to run the company." Joe looked to Tony. "Does that sound fair?"

Tony nodded. "That's right. If you win, it'll be between Joe and I."

"You said if I fall for Brooke. Define *fall for.*"

"The whole enchilada, Nick," Joe said. "Love, marriage and baby carriages."

Nick grinned. He'd never been in love before. He didn't think himself capable and marriage to any woman wasn't in his game plan. Ever. Just because the two of them found their so-called soul mates, didn't mean Nick wanted to follow in their footsteps. He wasn't like his brothers. He didn't do long-term relationships. "This is a piece of cake. You've got yourself a bet." Nick stood, eager to shake hands with his brothers and seal the deal. "And thanks for making this easy for me."

Joe looked at Tony and they both smiled smugly.

Nick would relish wiping the smiles off their faces and then he'd be off the hook to go about living his life. There was no way he'd let one woman and her child take him down.

No way in hell.

Five

The Lexus was a really great car, Brooke thought, running her hand along the smooth black leather seat. With dual temperature settings, a CD player and all the other bells and whistles, this was five-star luxury at its finest. She couldn't wait to get behind the wheel and take it for a drive. She sat in the passenger seat glancing at Nick behind the wheel as they drove to Dr. Maynard's office.

He wouldn't let her drive until she got the okay from the doctor this afternoon and she couldn't blame him for that. Still, she hated leaving Leah behind. Though she trusted Nurse Jacobs and Carlotta to watch her baby, she hadn't spent much time apart from her since the moment she'd been born.

"She's okay," Nick said, glancing at her. He had an uncanny way of knowing what she was thinking.

"I know. It's just that I feel lost without her."

"We'll get her a new car seat after your appointment, then you won't have to leave her behind again."

"Thanks for doing this, Nick."

"No problem. I've got a vested interest now." He winked.

She cocked him a wry smile. "I live to cook for you."

"That's the attitude," he said.

"So what would you like for dinner?"

"First, let's see what Steve says. If all is well, you can surprise me."

"All will be well."

Nick looked her up and down and the heat of his gaze made her quiver. "Looks good from where I'm sitting."

Brooke had to remind herself not to melt into a puddle just because he complimented her. It was Nick being Nick. She wouldn't fall for his charm again.

Thirty minutes later, after a thorough exam, Dr. Maynard gave her a clean bill of health. "I'm feeling so much better today," Brooke said, as he walked her out of the room.

"Good, well just take it slow for a while. Don't overdo anything," the doctor said.

"I won't."

Nick rose when Dr. Maynard walked her to the reception area. The two men shook hands.

"Well?" Nick asked her with a hopeful expression.

"I'm fine. I get to pass Go and collect two hundred dollars."

Nick smiled and his dimples appeared. She ignored them, telling herself the thrill she felt was only because she was finally back to square one and she could begin working on the house. Then she turned back to the doctor. "Oh, Dr. Maynard, can you recommend a pediatrician for Leah?"

"Sure can." He walked around to his reception desk,

pulled out a business card and handed it to her. "Dr. Natalie Christopher. She's excellent. And right in this building."

"Thanks for everything," Brooke said, glancing at the card. "I appreciate it."

"You take care now," he said to her, then turned to Nick. "I'll see you Friday."

Nick nodded and when he walked away, Brooke walked up to the desk and spoke to the receptionist, taking out her checkbook. "What do I owe you?"

The receptionist shook her head. "There's no charge."

"No charge? Really? But—"

Nick took her arm and led her away. "It's taken care of."

"You paid for me?"

"Not exactly. The doc owes me and he just settled up the score."

"What? I can't let you do that." Her voice elevated enough to cause stares from the patients in the waiting room.

"It's done, Brooke. Trust me. He's getting off cheap. Come on, we have to go car seat shopping."

Frustration rose and settled in her gut. She didn't want to make a scene in the waiting room, so she marched out of the office. She couldn't figure out why she was so angry with Nick. Ever since the accident, he'd been kind to her, so why did she want to lash out at him all the time? Was it because he could still push her internal buttons with a look or a smile? Was it because he was still the golden boy with all the money, good looks and charm one man could ask for? Or was it because he always seemed to be in control, always took care of things. He was someone she didn't want to rely on and yet, that's all she'd been doing lately was letting Nick make her life easy. It wouldn't last and she didn't want to get used to him being there for her. In the long run, she knew Nick couldn't be counted on.

Once they reached the parking lot, Nick took her hand and looked deep into her eyes. He was amazingly handsome and being near him complicated her life in ways she couldn't begin to deal with. She stilled from his touch, feeling a sharp jab of emotion, knowing she should pull her hand away.

"It's all yours," he said, dropping the keys into her palms.

Brooke stared down at the keys, speechless.

"You want to drive, don't you?" he asked softly.

Brooke nodded, holding back tears. Why had she gotten so emotional? Maybe, because Nick Carlino had just given her a car.

A car.

She wouldn't fool herself into thinking that her culinary skills could have earned her enough to pay for this car. This was the nicest, most decent thing anyone had ever done for her. Her lips quivered. *Don't cry, Brooke. Don't cry.*

But the more she tried to hold back, the more moisture pooled in her eyes. Then the dam broke and tears spilled down her cheeks.

Nick appeared puzzled, then he pulled her into his arms. "Hey," he said quietly, tucking her head under his chin. He stroked her back. "It's just a car."

"It's not just a car," she blubbered, feeling like a fool and hating Nick for being so sweet. Why on earth couldn't he just be the bastard she'd hated all these years and leave her alone?

She clung to him for an awkward minute then pulled away. "It's more than a car…it's safety for Leah and my future, and—"

"Don't cry," he said, lifting her chin and gazing at her. Her eyes were probably red and swollen, her nose all wet and ugly.

He bent his head and kissed her softly on the lips.

It was a warm, sweet, gentle brushing of the lips meant to console and comfort. It did just that, making Brooke feel safe and protected. She sighed deeply and allowed soft feelings for Nick to filter in, just this once. Fighting them would be futile, so she surrendered to her emotions and took what he offered.

When he lowered his head again, ready to do more consoling, Brooke's nerves rattled, not because she didn't want him to kiss her again, but because she did. She turned her head into his chest, denying another kiss, and announced with a whisper, "Men don't like seeing women cry. They think they've done something wrong and don't know how to fix it."

Nick cupped her chin gently and lifted her face to his. "Did I do something wrong?"

She shook her head. "No, you did something...nice."

His gaze lowered to her mouth. "And for the record, that's not why I kissed you."

She didn't want to know why he kissed her.

"I kissed you because you're a brave, honest woman who's been through a lot these past few days and..."

When he stopped speaking, Brooke searched his face, waiting. "And?"

Nick appeared slightly taken aback. He blinked and seemed a little flustered, then he moved away from her. "And, nothing. You looked like you needed a kiss, that's all." He headed for the passenger side of the car. "Are you ready to test this baby or what?"

Surprised by Nick's sudden change of demeanor, Brooke had no choice but to bolster her emotions. She took a deep, cleansing breath. "You bet. I'm ready."

She got into the car, put the key into the ignition and started the engine, then glanced at Nick. He looked at her oddly for a moment as if he were trying to figure something out, then he pointed to the road. "It's all yours, Brooke."

Sudden nerves took hold. Maybe she wasn't ready yet. Apprehension led to fear as she replayed the collision in her mind. The images rushed back to her fresh and vivid. She'd never been one for panic attacks, but she could see one happening now. "This is my first time behind the wheel since the accident."

"First times can be rough. Just do what comes naturally and you'll do fine." Nick sounded so confident.

"Really?" She nibbled on her lip.

"Gotta jump back onto that horse."

"I'm afraid of horses," she said.

Nick shook his head. "We'll remedy that another day. Right now, you're going to hold onto the steering wheel and put the car in gear, then gas it." He was back to being bossy again.

"Okay, don't go getting smug on me. I know *how* to drive."

Nick grinned. "That's my girl. Let's go."

Brooke pulled out of the parking lot and onto the road, doing what came naturally. Nick was right, she was doing fine. It was like riding a bike in some ways, everything seemed to come back to her and she'd overcome her initial fear.

"You've got it, Brooke," he said after a minute on the road.

"Thanks." She breathed a sigh of relief and wondered how she would have done without Nick sitting beside her, giving her courage. She felt more confident with each mile she drove. Now if she could only get the "that's my girl" comment out of her head, life would be peachy keen.

Nick helped Brooke install the car seat and was amazed at how intricate the danged thing was. Pull the strap here, tug there, make sure it fits tight enough and after all their struggles, Brooke finally said, "I'm going to have a professional look at it. Make sure it's safe."

"Doesn't look like it's going anywhere to me." He gave a final tug.

"Just to be sure," she said, staring at the car seat with concern. "Can't be too careful."

Brooke looked cute with her hair pulled back in a ponytail, her blonde curls falling past her shoulder, wearing an oversized T-shirt, jeans and flip-flops on her feet. She'd changed into different clothes once they'd returned home from Napa, calling them her "mommy clothes." It shouldn't be a turn-on, Nick was used to women in slinky clothes that left little to the imagination. But on Brooke, the clothes suited her and he found no matter what she wore, he was more than mildly interested.

"Thanks for helping me get it into the car," she said. "Maybe the experience will come in handy for you one day."

Nick winced. "I doubt it."

"You might change your mind. Don't be too sure of it, Nick." She glanced at her watch. "What time do you usually eat dinner?"

"I'm usually through working at seven."

"Okay, I'm going to surprise you tonight."

"You always do," he said and Brooke's soft laughter made him smile.

He thought back on their kiss this afternoon in the parking lot. That had been a surprise. It was nothing, something to soothe her fragile nerves, but he hadn't expected to be thrown for a loop by that kiss, or by holding her and bringing her comfort. Usually a master of self-control, Nick hadn't been able to stop himself and the rewards he'd reaped were those of protecting and calming her. It had felt good, damn good in a way he hadn't experienced before.

He scoffed silently at the notion. Just hours ago, he'd made the deal of all deals with his brothers. He was so certain he'd win his bet, that he'd started making plans for his return to Monte Carlo in the fall. He had a house there and planned on moving in permanently once the renovations were done, hopefully by late September.

By then, Tony and Rena would have their child. Joe would have married Ali, and Nick would be free to come and go as he pleased.

With no ties and no one to account to but himself.

Nick's stomach grumbled as he admitted to himself that he was ready for home cooking again. His mother had been a great cook and he remembered as a child being lured into the kitchen by pungent aromas of garlic and rosemary and bread baking in the oven. His mother would hum a melodic tune as she prepared the family meals, happy to be nourishing her young family. She'd been a saint to simmer Santo's volcanic nature. When Nick's mom was alive, the house had been a home. Nick had almost forgotten what that felt like.

He'd been smart to hire Brooke for the time being. He was really looking forward to sitting down to a meal that hadn't been boxed up, frozen or delivered from a local restaurant.

At least that was one craving Brooke could satisfy while under his roof.

"I guess it's time to say good-bye to Nurse Jacobs," Brooke said with a note of sadness. Brooke glanced down the driveway to where Leah was being strolled around the garden by her nurse. "She's a sweet woman."

"Are you sure you don't need her a little longer?" he asked.

"I'm sure," she said firmly. Bracing her hands on her hips next to the car, she hoisted her pretty chin. "I just drove you all over town. And installed my daughter's car seat. I'm fine, Nick."

"Correction, *we* installed the car seat."

"Fine, burst my bubble. *We* installed the car seat. But I really hate saying good-bye. And you know what's crazy? I don't even know her first name. She doesn't like it and wouldn't divulge it."

"It's Prudence. I was warned not to call her Pru, Prudy or Trudy. Otherwise, she might walk out."

Brooke's mouth gaped open for a second. Then she tossed her head back, giving way to spontaneous giggles that made Nick laugh too. She braced herself on the side of the car, her whole body jiggling as she tried to stifle her amusement.

Fully caught up in her laughter, Nick watched her breasts ride up and down her chest from underneath that loose shirt. He sidled next to her by the car. Her fresh citrus scent that reminded him of orange blossoms filled the air around her.

"I'm sorry," she said amid another round of giggles. "It just struck me as funny. You should have seen the look on your face when you were telling me that."

Nick smiled along with her. "Pretty unbelievable, isn't it?"

"Why didn't you tell me before now?"

"I forgot all about it. It was on the terms of her agreement."

"It's not a bad name at all," Brooke said, still smiling. Her entire face lit up when she was happy. "I don't know too many women who really like their name."

Nick tilted his head. "You don't like your name?"

She shook her head. "Not really. Brooke sounds so...I don't know, boring?"

"It suits you."

"So you think I'm boring?" Her amusement faded.

Nick winced. He'd stepped in it now. "Hell no. It's a strong name, like the woman. That's all I meant." He wouldn't tell her that her eyes reminded him of streaming clear aqua waters. What better name than Brooke?

Thankfully the conversation was interrupted when Nurse Jacobs approached with Leah in the stroller. "She's ready for a feeding."

"Okay," Brooke said, bending down to lift the baby out. "How's my pretty girl?" Brooke planted a kiss on Leah's forehead. "Did you like your walk?"

Leah clung tight to her mother, then focused her wide blue eyes his way and gave him a toothless smile.

Nick looked at mother and baby and an off-limits sign posted in his head.

"I'll take her inside and feed her, then I'll make dinner."

Brooke walked off with the baby and Nick stood in front of the house with the nurse. "As you know, Brooke got a clean bill of health from the doctor. I want to thank you for all you've done, and on such short notice."

"You're welcome. It was a treat for me too. I don't often get a chance to care for a young family. Leah's precious."

Nick nodded politely.

"Brooke is a determined young woman. It's a hard life, being a single mother. I hope she finds someone to share her life with." Nurse Jacobs cast him an assessing look. "You'll look out for her, won't you? As her friend?"

The "F" word. Brooke wouldn't want that label put onto their relationship. He didn't know how to label it, but they weren't friends. Exactly.

"She'll be working here for a while, so you don't have to worry," Nick replied, sounding as noncommittal as he could.

She nodded. "I'll go inside now and say my good-byes."

He shook her hand and thanked her once again, watching as she walked inside the house, leaving Nick alone with some nagging thoughts.

Brooke nursed Leah, knowing that pretty soon the pediatrician would probably encourage her to begin feeding the baby solid foods. Leah's appetite was growing and she was ready to have more substance in her diet. Brooke gazed down at her daughter—the bond they made through eye contact during this special time touched her heart. She'd miss these daily feedings, when she could forget all else, put her feet up and simply enjoy this special time with her baby.

Brooke's guilt came in sudden waves now when she thought about Leah's father. Her ex-husband didn't know he had a daughter. He didn't know Leah existed. Would it matter to him? A little voice in her head told her he had a right to know, but her fear had always won out. And if she were honest with herself, she'd have to admit that both fear and *anger* were at the root of her holding the truth from Dan.

Their marriage hadn't been perfect, but she would never have guessed that her husband was capable of such deception. Right under her nose, Dan had been carrying on an affair with another woman. He'd been sleeping with both of them.

She'd been blindsided by the betrayal and wasn't in any frame of mind to divulge her own pregnancy to him, not when he'd made it clear that he no longer loved her. But deep in her heart, Brooke knew she would have to confront him one day and reveal the truth to him. One day…but she didn't want that day to be anytime soon.

Brooke took Leah down to the kitchen and set her into her little playpen positioned by the granite island in the middle of the room. "Watch Mommy cook."

Leah looked up with wide curious eyes and picked up a pretzel-shaped teething ring and stuck it into her mouth. She gnawed on the ring with glee, as if it were a one-hundred dollar steak.

Brooke grinned. Her little girl would be cutting her first tooth soon.

"Okay, what shall we surprise Nick with?" Brooke scoured the refrigerator and pantry and decided on her meal. Cooking soothed her nerves. There was something therapeutic about producing a fine meal for someone who would appreciate it. She'd always enjoyed the nearly instant gratification she'd felt when it all came together better than expected. Working as a waitress while in high school, then managing the inn more recently, where she'd lend a hand in the kitchen, had taught her a thing or two about taste, presentation and nutrition.

By seven o'clock dinner was ready and the table was set. When Nick didn't appear, Brooke picked up Leah and went in search. She found him sitting in the downstairs study behind a desk, head deep in paperwork. The room was so masculine, with dark walnut panels combined with warm russet textured walls, massive bookcases and a wood-framed bay window that looked out to verdant vineyards, that Brooke felt uncomfortably out of place.

Leah's little baby sounds brought Nick's head up.

"Hi," she said, witnessing Nick's power and status once again, as he sat in the Carlino office. Sometimes, when he was adjusting her baby's car seat or holding Leah in his arms, she'd forget that he was a wealthy wine magnate with a vintage heritage that went back for generations. "Dinner is on the table."

"Okay, smells great from here." Nick rose and smiled at her. "What's for dinner?"

"It's a surprise. Come and see."

Nick followed her into the kitchen and she filled his plate and set it on the table. "Have a seat."

He glanced at the table set for one. "After you."

"What? No, Leah won't sit still. This is her fussy time. You eat. I'll have something later."

Nick glanced at the baby in her arms. She was peering straight at him with a look of contentment on her face.

Leah, don't make a liar out of your mommy.

"I'd like to have your company during dinner, Brooke. Set yourself a place."

"Why?"

"Why not? You have to eat too. Why should we both eat alone? Besides, how else can I critique your meals?"

"Oh, so you're going to rate my cooking."

"I'd like to *taste* your cooking. Are you going to sit or what?"

"You're grumpy when you're hungry." Brooke moved the playpen closer to the table and set Leah down, then dished herself a plate. She sat across from Nick and he watched her carefully. "Dig in," she said. "It's pork loin with tangy mango sauce. Cinnamon sweet potatoes and creamed spinach. Carlotta said you eat your salad last."

"I do."

"Why?"

"I like to get to the good stuff first," he said, casting her a look so hot, she could have burst into flames.

He dug into his food and Brooke waited patiently for a comment.

"You gonna eat or watch me clean my plate?" he asked after about a minute.

She passed him the basket of warm Italian bread she'd sliced and toasted under the broiler then coated with olive pesto. "I can do both, you know."

Nick looked at her with admiration. He pointed with his fork to what was left on his plate. "This is delicious."

She breathed a sigh of relief. "Carlotta said it was one of your favorites."

"Yeah, but I've never tasted anything this good."

"Helps when you have an amazing kitchen to work with. And good cuts of meat."

Nick shook his head. "You never could take a compliment."

"I didn't get that many from you," she blurted.

Nick smiled. "Now who's grumpy?"

Brooke clamped her mouth shut, hating that she made a reference to their past. She wanted no reminders of that time in her life.

Nick got another plate of food and demolished it before Brooke had a chance to finish her first helping.

"It was hard to say good-bye to Nurse Jacobs." She took a small bite of her potatoes.

"Was it? She could have stayed on longer."

"It wasn't necessary. I'm feeling fine. It's just that I've never really remained in one place long enough to have a lot of close friends. She and I sort of bonded. I'm hoping now that I'm in Napa for good, I'll be able to make some friends."

Leah fussed and Brooke put down her fork to lift her out of the playpen. "You want outta there, baby girl, don't you?"

She set Leah on her lap and continued with her meal while Nick looked on. "I've left another message with Molly and I hope she calls me back. I'd like to reconnect with her. Not that I won't have enough to keep me busy," she said as she tried the spinach. Leah's hand came up and she grabbed the fork from her and giggled. "Leah!"

The next time she tried to get a forkful into her mouth, Leah twisted in her lap, squirming so much that Brooke had to put her silverware down. "What, you want to play now?"

She was just about to stand up, when Nick reached for Leah. "Here, let me have her. Finish your meal, Brooke."

Leah went willingly to Nick, nearly bounding out of Brooke's arms and into his. Leah adjusted herself onto his chest and settled in, her small body against Nick's strong chest. Brooke's heart gave way a little.

"Let your mama finish her meal," he said in a stern tone and when Leah twisted her face, ready to let go big tears, Nick softened his voice. "Okay, okay, Leah." Then he bounced her on his knee.

Brooke smiled wide and Nick shot her an annoyed look. "What? You think I don't know how to bounce a kid on my knee?"

"I didn't say a word." Brooke finished her meal with her head down, refusing to give in to the tender emotions that washed over her as Nick consoled her baby daughter, speaking softly and charming her with sweet words.

That night, Brooke had a slight argument with Nick over their sleeping arrangements on their way upstairs. She wanted to give him his room back, since she'd be staying on for weeks. But Nick wouldn't budge claiming she needed the extra space for the baby's things and the guest room had everything he needed for the time being.

Stubbornly, she wasn't ready to give up until Nick walked over to her in the hallway near the master suite, ready to compromise. "Or we could *share* my room," he suggested with an arch of his brow. He began taking his shirt off.

Brooke froze on the spot, watching one button after another open to his tanned chest. She was very much aware that they were alone in the house. Carlotta, much to her surprise, didn't live in the house. She used a downstairs room for sleeping when the Carlinos had a big party or special occasion; otherwise she went home before dark to spend time with her husband. "Fine, you made your point. I'll take your room. Th-thank you."

Nick backed away then, satisfied.

She entered her room and closed the door. After she bathed Leah and nursed her one last time before putting her to bed, she took a long hot soak in the bathtub and fell into a gloriously deep sleep.

Brooke woke in a great mood. She fixed Nick a breakfast of bacon and eggs and home-fried potatoes, grabbing a quick plate for herself before heading out. Nick had called Randy, arranging for Brooke to drive by his shop this morning so he could double-check the car seat for Leah. Randy had been nice enough to make a few adjustments and she drove away relieved to know Leah was as safe as she possibly could be. Still, Brooke drove five miles under the speed limit all the way to the house, garnering some dirty looks from the drivers behind her.

"Here it is, sweet girl," she said once they arrived. "This is our new home."

Brooke spent the better part of the day making assessments and writing up a list of all the repairs she'd need, setting her priorities. Yesterday, she'd called to have the electricity turned on, and that made her work much easier. She noted the sizes of the beds in each room and checked the bed linens in the closets. There were antique quilts that she could have cleaned but the bed sheets and all the towels would have to be replaced. Thankfully, the kitchen appliances were in working order, though on the old side, their dated look added charm to the kitchen. The dining room was full of dust and debris but the table and chairs were made of fine wood that would polish up nicely.

Brooke contacted a few local handymen and painters in the area by phone and set up appointments, then she called to make Leah an appointment with the pediatrician. She also placed another call to Molly Thornton, hoping her friend was still living in Napa.

She felt an odd sense of belonging here. She'd never owned a home of her own. Even the house she'd shared with Dan had been a rental. At least during their quickie divorce, she didn't have to deal with property settlements; he'd taken what was his and she'd taken what was hers.

But this house was all hers and an overwhelming sense of pride coursed through her system. Tears pooled in her eyes as she looked around the old house, seeing it not as it stood today, but envisioning how it would be one day. Her dream was finally coming true and it had been a long road getting here. Often she'd wondered if this was her aunt's way of making up to Brooke for what her father had done to her. Nothing really could. How can you make up for a man who'd abandoned his family?

But she was grateful for her aunt's generosity. Because of her, Brooke would secure a future for Leah without any outside help. If she didn't rely on anyone, then she couldn't be disappointed. Her ex-husband had taught her that hard lesson.

Yet it was Nick's face that had popped into her mind. It was so unexpected that her breath caught in her throat. Why had she been thinking of Nick? Was it because he'd disappointed her once, or was it because she wanted to make sure he wouldn't have the chance to disappoint her ever again?

"I don't know about him, Leah," she said, sweeping up her daughter and planting kisses on her cheek. Leah was fascinated by her new surroundings and had been quietly curious since they'd arrived, letting Brooke make her phone calls without interruptions.

By mid-morning, Brooke had accomplished what she'd hoped to and decided a trip into town was necessary. She packed up Leah and made their first stop at a hardware store to pick up cleaning supplies, some small appliances and a beginner's tool kit. Next she went to Baby Town to purchase a new playpen for Leah that she could keep in their house, eliminating the need for her to continually cart it back and forth. After picking out a jungle-themed playpen, she drove to the grocery store and bought beverages and food to stock in the kitchen. It was a funny thing, just having milk and bread in the refrigerator made her happy. She smiled the entire way home.

Hours later Brooke glanced at her watch to find it was time to head back to Nick's house. The time had flown by and she was extremely happy with her progress. She'd managed to clean up the refrigerator, wash the kitchen floors and counters and arrange a new toaster, food processor and coffeemaker in strategic places in the kitchen. She'd had a full day and now was off to make dinner for Nick.

She arrived a little later than she'd planned, so dinner was a rush of getting Leah nursed and down for a nap, and creating something wonderful to eat. The something wonderful ended up being a quick stir-fry with shrimp and scallops, scallions, and veggies over brown rice.

"I know I must look a mess," she offered when she heard Nick walk into the kitchen, precisely at seven. "And dinner's going to be a little late today." Steam from the wok rose up and heated her face. She wiped her forehead with her arm, feeling like a slug from the earth. She hadn't had a chance to change her clothes or clean up before starting dinner. "Give me a second and I'll have it all ready."

Nick approached her in a slow easy stride. "Why, do you have somewhere you need to be?"

She snapped her head up. Heavens, he looked like a zillion bucks today. His tan trousers and a chocolate brown shirt brought out the bronze of his skin and accented those dark blue eyes. His appearance made her feel even more a mess, if that were possible. She caught the subtle scent of his musky cologne and knew immediately it probably cost more than her entire wardrobe at the moment. "No, of course not. I'm sorry I'm running late."

She took the wooden spoon and stirred, as if that would make the dinner cook faster.

Nick sidled up next to her and covered her hand with his. Stir-fry steam continued to drift into her face, but that wasn't what caused her body to flame. Having his hands on her was doing a great job of that.

"There's no rush," he said quietly and her heart pounded in her chest. He stroked her gently and she didn't dare look at his face and show him the turmoil he caused her. Instead, she focused and took a deep breath.

"Brooke?"

"What?" she barked out and Nick smiled.

He took the spoon from her and shut off the burner on the stove. "Don't make yourself crazy about this, honey. If you're running late, just tell me. I'm a big boy, I can wait for dinner."

"You said seven."

"Or later. Today it's going to be later. Go up and take a minute for yourself."

"Is that your way of telling me I look like something the cat dragged in?"

"You look fine, Brooke. You've had a busy day. And I want to hear all about it."

"You do?"

He nodded.

She glanced at Leah asleep in her little playpen. "But Leah's down here."

"I've got some reading to do. I'll stay in here and watch her."

Nick had a determined look in his eyes and she decided to take him up on his offer, rather than argue about it. "Okay, I'll be down in a few minutes."

She raced upstairs and tossed off her clothes, jumped into the shower and reveled in the refreshing spray that not only cleansed her, but relaxed her as well. She changed into a pair of clean jeans and a black sleeveless tunic and brushed her hair back, away from her face, letting it fall in curls down her back. Taking a look in the mirror, she liked this image reflecting back at her much better than the harried, uptight woman she'd been just twenty minutes ago.

When she entered the kitchen again, she found Nick standing over Leah's playpen, watching her sleep. The moment caught her by surprise. She walked over to stand beside him and they stood there silently like that for a few seconds.

Finally, Nick looked at her. "She made some sounds. I thought she was waking up."

"Those are her baby noises. She's not a quiet sleeper. You'll get used to it."

Nick glanced once more at Leah, then took a long assessing look at her. "Feel better?"

"Much."

The appreciation in Nick's eyes told her he liked what he

saw. Her nerves went raw and she resumed her position at the stove to finish cooking the meal and ignore the flutters threatening to ruin her dinner.

Nick set the table, putting out plates and utensils and Brooke opened her mouth to stop him but then clamped it shut again. He'd said it point-blank tonight—he was a big boy. If he wanted to set his table who was she to tell him not to?

So she sliced bread and stirred the meal as Nick set the table and Leah slept. For anyone walking in on the three of them in the kitchen, they'd think it a homey domestic scene. Only it wasn't, and Brooke had to remind herself that Nick was her employer and she was leaving him as soon as humanly possible.

Nick ate every bite on his plate and went to the stove to get a second helping. When he sat down again, instead of diving into his food, he leaned back in his seat looking her over. "So how did it go today?" He poured himself a glass of wine and gestured for her, but she shook her head. She couldn't drink alcohol while nursing her baby.

"You really want to know?" She didn't think her day would be of any consequence to him, but if he'd rather make small talk than eat then she would oblige.

"I wouldn't have asked if I didn't want to know." He sipped his white zinfandel thoughtfully.

"I got a lot accomplished. Actually, I'm feeling pretty good about things," and Brooke went on to explain the details of her day. To her surprise, Nick asked quite a few questions and seemed genuinely interested in her progress. In fact she felt so comfortable discussing the subject with him, she asked him for advice. "I was hoping you could help me figure out a good promotional plan to advertise and attract guests, once I get my place ready."

Nick thought for a second, scratching his jaw. "I've made a lot of contacts in the area. I'm sure I could call in some favors."

"I wasn't asking for your help, just a point in the right direction."

"Right, heaven forbid I should help you."

Nick focused his attention on her face then lowered his gaze to her chest and the hint of cleavage her top revealed. He didn't seem to mind that she'd caught him in the act. He merely sipped his wine and continued to look at her until heat crawled up her neck.

"I appreciate you will—"

"Get your place registered with tour books and guides. You'll need a Web site. You'll also need to work out arrangements with other bed-and-breakfasts so that they refer tourists to you if they can't accommodate them. Initially, I'd say to visit local wineries and make your place known. Carlino Wines will put you on top of our referral list for visitors." Through tight lips, he added, "Unless that's against your rules too."

Brooke took offense to that. "I don't have rules, Nick."

He finished off his wine and poured another glass. "Sure you do. You don't want anything from me."

"I don't want anything from any man," she said, her anger rising. She was sorry she'd asked him for advice. "It's not personal."

His brow furrowed. "Is that because of what happened between us in high school?"

Brooke had heard enough. She rose from her seat and took up her plate, unable to hide her annoyance. "Maybe you don't know this, but there is *life* after Nick."

Nick shot up and followed her to the sink. "What is it then? Why are you so damn stubborn? Is it your ex? Did he do a number on you?"

She winced at the mention of her ex. "I don't want to talk about it."

"Hell, maybe you should. Maybe it'll knock off that chip on your shoulder."

She whirled around and faced him straight on. "I don't have a chip on my shoulder. I have a baby to raise by myself and I'm trying my best not to get hurt again. That's all, no chip, just survival. But you wouldn't understand that."

"Yeah, because I've got everything I want."

"Hell, it looks like it from where I'm standing!"

Nick ignored her accusation and wouldn't let up. "Tell me. What did he do to you, Brooke? Why isn't he around for Leah?"

Brooke's defenses fell at the mention of her daughter. Emotion roiled in the pit of her stomach making her queasy. Her heart ached for Leah and all that she'd lost. Dan's betrayal had cut her to the core, because it meant her daughter wouldn't know her own father. It meant, when she did tell Dan about his daughter, he might not care to know her. He might abandon Leah, the way he'd abandoned Brooke. And that would be too much to take. Too hard to deal with.

Brooke lashed out at Nick because he was there, and because he'd asked for the truth. "He isn't around for Leah, because he doesn't know about Leah! One week before I found out I was pregnant, Dan came to me with the news that he was having an affair. She was pregnant with his child. He left me and the child he'd didn't know about. And," she said, her tone and bravado fading, "my beautiful baby girl isn't anyone's castaway. She isn't." Tears spilled down her cheeks and she let them fall freely, shedding her heartache with each stinging drop. "She'll never be. And when I tell Dan about her, it'll kill me if he hurts her the way he hurt me."

Nick ran a hand through his hair. "Christ, Brooke," he said in a low rasp.

"I know," she said, between sobs. She swatted at her shoulder. "Knocked the chip right off."

Nick closed his eyes briefly, then grabbed her around the waist and drew her into his chest. She wound her arms around him and sobbed quietly while he held her, making her feel safe and protected.

"Damn him," he muttered. "The jerk."

"I know," Brooke replied over and over again. "I know. I know."

"Want me to have him killed?"

Even through her heartache, she chuckled. "How would you do it?"

"He would just disappear one day, never to be heard from again."

Brooke nestled into his chest a little more. "I appreciate the thought," she whispered.

"I'm a helluva guy."

"Don't be nice to me, Nick," she pleaded.

"Don't be so damn brave and beautiful and sexy."

"I'm none of those things." She wasn't. She was just muddling her way through life, making mistakes and trying to cope the best way she knew how.

Nick lifted her chin and met her eyes. "You're all of those things, Brooke." Then he lowered his head and kissed her.

It wasn't a consoling kiss, but an all-out Nick Carlino kiss filled with demand and passion. He cupped her face, weaving fingers into her hair and tilted her head to get a better angle, then he kissed her again, his mouth hot and moist and intoxicating. Brooke fell into the sensations swirling down her body in a spiral of heat.

He pressed her mouth open and drove his tongue inside,

taking her into a more intimate place—a place Brooke hadn't been in a long time.

She wanted more. She wanted *him* but she knew it would have to stop. She couldn't do this. Not with Nick. Those thoughts turned to mush when he drizzled kisses down her throat and cupped her breasts with his hands. He groaned with need and backed her up against the counter, their bodies hard and aching for each other. His thumbs stroked over her blouse, making her nipples peak, tormenting her with slow circles that sent shockwaves down her body.

It felt good to be kissed this way by Nick, to have him desire her, and she would die a happy woman if he made love to her now. But Brooke thought about Leah again, and the mistakes she'd already made in her life.

Nick would be another one. And she couldn't afford that luxury.

"No, Nick." She broke off his kiss, and regretted it immediately, but she was determined to stop him. "We can't do this."

He gazed at her with smoky eyes that promised a hot night between the sheets. His hands were halfway up her blouse. He removed them and waited.

"I haven't had sex in a long time," she confessed.

"You haven't forgotten anything."

She squeezed her eyes shut for a moment. "You're good at bringing it all back."

"Somehow I don't think that's an invitation."

"It's not. It's an explanation of why I let things get out of control. My life is complicated right now."

Nick sighed. "Sex doesn't have to be."

She breathed in deep and his scent on her lingered. "I'm not ready."

Nick backed up and gave her breathing room. "When

you are, you have an open invitation. You know where my room is."

She swallowed past the lump in her throat and nodded.

They stared at each other a long moment, then Nick turned away, picked up his keys and walked out the front door.

Brooke stood there, bracing herself against the granite counter, her body aching for completion. She needed the physical act, but she also needed the intimacy of being held and loved and cared for. She wanted the bond and connection that lovemaking at its finest could bring. Knowing she had an open invitation with Nick rattled her nerves and made her imagine things she shouldn't be imagining.

When Leah stirred, Brooke glanced down to watch her daughter's eyes open to the world, her blond curls framing her chubby cheeks and a little pout forming on her mouth. She believed with her whole heart that she'd done the right thing by pushing Nick away tonight.

For all three of them.

Six

The week flew by uneventfully. Brooke got into a routine of waking early enough to cook breakfast and get out the door by nine to work at the house. She'd come back to the Carlino estate in the late afternoon to shower and make dinner. All in all it was working out better than she'd hoped.

Nick came and went as he pleased, and she was grateful there was no tension between them. At least not on the surface. They'd share their meals, talk about their day and have a few laughs. After dinner, they'd head in opposite directions.

She didn't think about Nick during working hours, when her focus was on getting the place cleaned up. She had a handyman there during the week, fixing doors and repairing damage to the walls as well as bolstering the railings that wrapped around the house on three sides. The painters were due next week and Brooke had to begin building a website for her project. She could write the text herself, but she couldn't add photos until the house transformed from the deteriorating Addams Family house to one that looked appealing and inviting. She'd made plans to visit wineries in the area this weekend, reacquainting herself with local vintners and getting the word out about her new establishment.

That would be the hardest part. She'd never felt as though she belonged in Napa and during the night she struggled with old feelings of not being good enough and of not fitting in—only this time, she was able to talk herself out of those nagging thoughts. She'd come a long way since her teen years, having been through some rough patches and learning from them. This was her chance for independence and happiness.

But while she could talk herself out of those old feelings, new feelings had emerged that were harder to keep down. At night, she'd lie across her bed and think about the temptation that lay just a few steps away. Nick had let her know in no uncertain terms that he was available to her if she wanted him. She had an open invitation. And every night since, she'd thought about his offer and him and what it would be like making love to Nick.

The passion they experienced in the kitchen in those few unguarded minutes had been two-sided. She'd opened up to Nick and bared her soul to him and he'd understood her pain. He'd approached her not from self-fulfilling lust, but from shared desire. Each night, as she turned down her covers and crawled into bed, she'd secretly wished Nick was beside her and as the nights wore on, it was getting harder and harder to sleep knowing what she craved, if just in body, was so close to her.

And yet, never further out of her reach.

That afternoon, Brooke stopped work early, deciding Leah needed a break from the drudgery of the old house.

As much as she wanted to accomplish her tasks as soon as possible, she never wanted to lose sight of Leah's needs. She'd stopped off at the store and bought Leah a turtle-shaped inner tube and a two-piece pink bathing suit. Leah loved water, her bath time being one of her favorite activities. Today, they were going for a swim in the Carlino pool.

"Oh, don't you look sweet in your new suit," she said as she dressed her daughter on Nick's big bed. She adjusted the straps on Leah's two-piece swimsuit. "There, all set." Leah giggled and kicked her legs up. "Let's go. Mr. Turtle wants to take you for a ride."

Brooke wore her own two-piece suit covered by a sundress. She grabbed the already inflated turtle—a bad move on her part, she should have blown it up downstairs—picked up the diaper bag full of towels, sunscreen, bottled water, Leah's hat as well as her diapers, then lifted Leah up in her other arm. "Here we go, little girl."

She made it out the door and headed toward the staircase, balancing baby and everything else in her arms, precariously.

"Need some help?" Nick strolled out of his bedroom and didn't wait for an answer. He slipped his hands into the straps of the diaper bag, taking it from her, then lifted Mr. Turtle off her shoulder. "Did you load the diaper bag down with lead?" he asked.

"Not quite," she said, and a chuckle escaped. "It's just a girl thing. Thanks."

Nick followed her down the stairs. "I take it Leah likes water."

"We'll see. She's never been in a pool like this before."

"Really? This I've got to see."

"What are you doing home?" she asked matter-of-factly. It was his home and he could come and go whenever he pleased, but Brooke was really looking forward to having this special time alone with Leah. And if she were honest, she didn't really want to parade around in her swimsuit with Nick looking on. Her body wasn't perfect, not in the way Nick was accustomed to seeing a woman—she had stretch marks still in the process of fading that never really bothered her until now.

Suddenly, the idea of using the Carlino pool lost its appeal, but she couldn't back out now without looking like a complete idiot. Besides, Leah deserved some splash and play time.

Suck it up, Brooke.

"I only work half a day on Friday. It's a guy thing," he said with a wink. "Maynard wiggled out of our tennis game, claiming he had a patient in need." A wry grin spread across his face. "A likely story. He didn't want to get beat again."

"Yeah, and owe you any more favors like treating me for free."

Nick only smiled.

Once they reached the pool, Nick set her things down on the chaise lounge. The day was gloriously warm, the sky a clear blue and the pungent scent of new grapes nurtured on the vine filled the air.

Brooke laid out her towels on the chair, then set Leah down and lathered her with sunscreen before plunking a pink bonnet on her head. "I called Dr. Christopher today and she said Leah could be out in the sun for thirty minutes as long as she was protected."

Nick took a seat in an adjoining chaise lounge and spread his legs out. He was dressed in slacks and a white button-down shirt with the sleeves rolled up. "You're a good mother," he said and she waited for the punch line, but when none came she realized he'd meant it.

"Thank you." She stepped out of her flip-flops. "I never thought I'd be a single mom." She shimmied off her sundress and let it pool down her legs. Then stepping away, she reached down to pick up Leah and the turtle tube.

When she finally glanced at Nick, she found he'd put on sunglasses, which was a good thing because now she couldn't see his eyes measuring her. Thankfully, her suit wasn't a bikini thong. She'd picked out a more conservative two-piece suit, yet there was more skin exposed than she'd like Nick to see.

"I like the suit," he commented immediately.

It suddenly got ten degrees warmer under the direct sun. "I, uh…it's nothing special."

"Leah could be a model for *Baby News* in that pink getup."

Oh, he meant Leah. Now, Brooke wanted to die of mortification.

She turned away and took her first step into the pool. The water felt cool enough to be refreshing, but warm enough to enjoy.

"Brooke?"

She tossed the turtle into the water and watched it land with a little splash in the shallow end. Then she turned to face him, holding Leah close in her arms.

"Your kid looks cute, but I was complimenting you."

"Let's just leave it at, Leah looks cute." Brooke took another step in, and then another. Normally, she wasn't the wait and see type of swimmer—she loved to dive in and feel the unexpected shock of the water, but of course she couldn't do that now. Once she got in up to her waist, she splashed water on her daughter's legs. Leah bent down to touch it. Her chubby fingers reached out again and again and Brooke had to cling onto her tight for fear of dropping her.

Nick sat forward, straddling the lounge, and tipped his sunglasses down. "She's fidgeting again."

Brooke tossed her head back and laughed. "Now I've got you saying words like fidgeting."

Nick smiled and those dimples popped out and caught sunlight. "I guess you do."

He leaned back in his lounge, getting comfortable as Brooke finally managed to get Mr. Turtle to accept Leah's weight. Once she was sitting on the floatation device comfortably, Brooke breathed easier. She pushed Leah around and around, her daughter's big smiles and cackles of delight warming Brooke's heart.

Then a thought struck and she hated to ask, but she also hated to miss this moment. "Nick, a big favor? Since it's Leah's first time in a pool, will you take a picture of her?"

He narrowed his eyes as he made his way over. "Depends, what are you feeding me tonight?"

"Anything you'd like. Name it."

"I'll let you know later. Where's the camera?"

"In the diaper bag."

Nick sorted through her things and came up with the camera. She didn't have to instruct him how to use it—he seemed knowledgeable. He asked for smiles, and Leah obliged immediately, staring straight at Nick. He bent down close to the steps and clicked off a few shots.

"You look hot," Brooke blurted, noticing beads of sweat on his brow.

Nick cast her a charming grin. "I'm taking that as a compliment."

"You know what I mean," she said, spinning Leah around on the tube again.

"Do you swim?" he asked.

Brooke glanced with longing at the long kidney-shaped pool. "Like a fish. I'm a good swimmer."

"Hang on. I'll be right back."

A few minutes later, she heard a quiet splash from behind and turned toward the deep end. Nick swam underwater the length of the pool and came up just inches from her and Leah.

Leah's eyes rounded and she clapped her hands with glee when she saw Nick. He patted her on the head and she followed the course of his hands, watching his every move with fascination. "I'll watch her for a few minutes. Take a swim."

"You don't have to do that." Brooke stood close enough to Nick to reach out and touch the droplets of water trickling down his chin onto his chest. His dark hair was pushed off his face and she noted a small scar cutting into his forehead she didn't know he had. It was just enough of a flaw on a perfectly handsome face to make him look dangerously sexy. Brooke figured it safer to take him up on his offer than stand in the shallow end drooling over a well-muscled hard body.

"Have at it, Brooke," he commanded, pointing to the water. He grabbed hold of the turtle tube and gently pushed it through the water. "The kid and I will be just fine. When you get done, I have a favor to ask you."

"Ah, that makes more sense. You have an ulterior motive."

Their eyes met with amusement.

Brooke turned to kiss her daughter's cheek. "Watch Mommy swim."

"Don't worry," Nick said with a sinister arch to his brow. "We will."

Brooke turned and dove into the water, freeing herself from all worries and simply enjoying her swim. She lapped the pool several times, slicing through the clean rejuvenating water with her breaststroke and several minutes later, she came up to take a breather on the opposite end of the pool.

With a hand on the edge, she glanced at Leah, who was now out of Mr. Turtle and being swirled around by Nick. He held her under her arms and lifted her high in the air, then lowered her feet into the water, letting her kick and splash before lifting her high again. Next, he twirled her around above the water, holding her like a little horizontal helicopter then swooped her down again to let her feet and legs splash through the water.

Leah loved it. Her joyous cackling tore into Brooke's heart. The scene they made, the way her daughter looked at Nick—it was almost more than she could bear to watch.

She swam over to them and Nick turned to her as she straightened up to face him with Leah clinging to his neck.

"She's a swimmer, just like her mama," he said. "Did you enjoy your swim?"

"It was very refreshing."

"For me, too. It isn't every day that I have a gorgeous dripping wet blonde standing in front of me."

Brooke ignored his comment, but it was hard to ignore the earnest expression on his face. "Thanks for the swim. I enjoyed it. Here," she said, reaching for Leah. "I'll take her now."

Nick tried to untangle Leah's arms from around him, but she didn't want to let go. Brooke coaxed her with another ride in Mr. Turtle. After she set her into it and moved her to and fro, she turned to Nick. "You said you had a favor to ask?"

Nick sat down on the pool's step and stretched out his long legs, his face lifted to the sun. "My sister-in-law, Rena, is dying to meet you. Well, actually, she's dying to see Leah and pick your brain about babies and labor and everything else." Then he met her eyes. "My brother Tony said she's going stir-crazy. She's as big as a house, but don't tell her I said that. And she wants a night out. I invited them to dinner tomorrow night."

"That sounds okay," she said with reluctance. She didn't want to enmesh herself any more into Nick's life than necessary.

Nick picked up on her reluctance. "I know it's Saturday night. If you had plans—"

"I'm a single mom with a five-month-old baby. Not exactly hot date material, Nick. I'll cook for your family."

"I wasn't suggesting that. We'll go out for dinner. And then come back here for drinks, maybe some of that blueberry pie you made the other day."

"I don't have a sitter for Leah."

"Not a problem. She'll come along."

Fully surprised by the suggestion, Brooke tossed her head back and a deep rumble of laughter spilled out. "You can't be serious."

"Why not?" Nick looked truly puzzled.

"Leah will disrupt everyone's meal. You see how *fidgety* she is, especially if she's not in her own surroundings."

"So? It'll show Rena and Tony what they're in for." His grin was a little too smug.

"As in, it serves them right for having a baby?" Brooke wasn't sure she liked Nick's suggestion to use Leah as a means to taunt his brother.

"It's not really Tony's baby. At least not biologically, but he's in it for the long haul and no one could be happier about becoming a father than Tony. He'll love meeting Leah. Both of them will and it'll get them off my back. They've been hounding me all week about you."

Brooke's internal alarm sounded. "They don't think that you and I are, uh…"

Those dimples popped out with his sly smile. "You can set them straight."

"Darn right I will."

It shouldn't matter to her what Nick's brother thought about their living arrangements, but it did. She had a good deal of pride. She wasn't one of Nick's bimbo girlfriends that he could toss aside when he was done. She'd never put herself in that position.

"I'll take that as a yes."

"Okay, I'll go to dinner." Did she really have a choice without coming off as sounding ungrateful? She recalled all the questions she had before Leah was born and how nice it would have been to talk to a friend who had gone through it already. And since Molly hadn't returned her calls, Brooke didn't have any female companionship in Napa aside from Carlotta, who seemed to be on the opposite schedule from hers. When Brooke was home, Carlotta wasn't working and vice versa.

Nick's comment about the parentage of Rena's baby spiked her curiosity. She'd left Napa and never looked back and apparently, a good deal had happened during that time. "Is there anything I should know about Tony and Rena, just so I don't put my foot in it?"

Nick shrugged. "The short story is Rena was married to Tony's best friend. Right before David died, Tony promised him he'd take care of Rena and the baby."

"How tragic. She lost a husband and he lost his best friend."

"Yeah, it was rough, but Tony and Rena had past history and my brother worships his wife. They're one of the few happily married couples I know."

"Does the *long* story have something to do with your father?"

Nick drew in a sharp breath and uncharacteristic pain crossed his face. "Santo had a hand in ruining lives and Tony and Rena were drawn into all that."

Leah squawked, letting go a little cry of complaint. Brooke wanted to hear more about Tony and Rena, but it was time to get out of the water. She lifted Leah off the float. "I think it's time to get out or my little girl will turn into a prune. She's ready for a nap."

Nick stepped out first and wrapped a towel around Leah. Together they wiped her down, before he stepped away. "Thanks," she said. It was a simple gesture that lasted no more than a few seconds, but being here with Nick, doing things together was starting to get too comfortable and feel too right.

When Brooke knew in her heart it was all wrong.

Nick hated to admit how much he was looking forward to having dinner with Brooke tonight. Whenever he thought about her, it was with a smile. She made him laugh and he enjoyed her company more than any other female he had or hadn't been sleeping with. She was off-limits in so many ways, yet he found himself drawn to her. Part of that was due to the challenge she posed. She didn't want him and she'd made that clear.

She was also at the root of the deal he'd made with his brothers.

Falling for Brooke was a deal breaker and Nick didn't like to lose.

He showered, shaved and combed his hair, then dressed in a pair of casual beige trousers and a black shirt. They agreed on having an early dinner because of Leah's schedule and so Nick knocked on Brooke's door at precisely six in the evening.

"I'll be right there," she said, her voice hurried. She yanked open the door and rushed off, putting earrings on as she moved to the bed. "Leah took a longer nap today and I'm running late."

She dashed about the room, tossing a few things in the diaper bag and checking on her own purse. While standing before him in a knockout black dress that hugged her curves and reached her knees, she slipped her feet into heels. "I'm sorry."

"Don't be. I'm enjoying the show."

She glanced at him and rolled her eyes, too harried to see his humor. "Okay, what do you need me to do?"

"Stop teasing me, for one," she said.

"Done. What else?"

"Leah needs to be fed."

Nick shrugged, blinking, recalling the time in the hospital when he'd witnessed Brooke feeding her baby. "Sorry, can't help you with that."

"Sure you can." She grabbed a bottle out of her diaper bag and shoved it into his hand. "Give her this. She'll do the rest. She'll take enough to last her until tonight. It'll keep her content through dinner."

Nick sat on the bed and she put Leah into his arms. "Here you go. I've got to comb my hair."

"It's okay if we're a few minutes late you know."

"Good to know," she called out. "Because we will be."

A chuckle rumbled in his chest at her answer. Then he looked down at Leah who seemed happy enough at the moment. "You want this?" he asked. Her big hazel eyes followed the bottle until Nick got it near her mouth. She grabbed hold and tipped it until the thin milky fluid flowed into her mouth. She sucked in a steady rhythm and Nick watched as she drank.

Leah kept her gaze focused onto his eyes as she drained the bottle, her little chubby cheeks working for all she was worth. "You like that, don't you," he said quietly, getting the hang of it. Leah made it easy. She'd taken to him from the moment he'd wrestled her out of the car seat after the accident.

"She looks pretty," he called out, thinking it wasn't a lie. Leah had golden curls, big eyes, rosy cheeks and Brooke had dressed her in a sunny yellow dress that made her look like a sunflower.

Brooke walked out of the bathroom, appearing beautiful and calmer, her blond hair curling past her shoulders in waves and her smile lighting up the room. "Thank you. Compliments to my daughter will always win you points."

"I'll remember that," Nick said, taking a leisurely look at her. "How about compliments to you?"

"I don't count."

"You do to me," Nick blurted, then stood with Leah in his arms, surprising himself for his uncanny appraisal of both of them. "Like mother, like daughter. You both look amazing tonight."

"Thank you," Brooke said slowly, refusing him eye contact. She reached for the baby. "I'll take Leah if you wouldn't mind taking the diaper bag."

"Got it. Toss me your keys. I'll drive. I hope you like Italian. We're going to Alfredo's. We own half the place so there won't be much chance of Leah getting us thrown out."

"Funny, Nick. You'll see. She can be quite a handful. And for the record, I *love* Italian."

Twenty minutes later, Nick walked into the restaurant

holding the handle of the car seat that transformed into Leah's baby seat. Brooke was by his side carrying Leah. "Oh I forgot to tell you, my brother Joe invited himself to dinner and he's bringing his fiancée."

Nick knew Joe and Tony were conspiring against him, trying their damnedest to bring Brooke and him together for their own reasons. Nick was slightly amused at their efforts. He was a worthy opponent and while he might be a sucker for blondes with big eyes and pretty smiles, he wasn't a fool. He might want Brooke in his bed, but that's where it would end.

His brothers underestimated him if they thought they would win their bet.

Brooke glanced at him. "Is this the whole family?"

"Except for a few cousins on my mother's side, living in Tuscany, yeah. This would have been the end of the Carlino line, except now Tony is having a boy."

"I'd like a boy one day," Brooke said quietly and he noted a sense of defeat in her tone. "It's lonely being an only child. I wanted Leah to have a brother or sister."

"Maybe one day you'll get your wish."

Brooke shook her head. "No. That's an impossibility." Her gaze flowed over Leah with softness in her eyes. "Leah's enough."

Nick didn't pursue it. He never talked to women about having babies. He didn't care to know their dreams and hopes for the future because it would never include him. He was destined to be the family's favorite uncle. And that suited him just fine.

Tony and Rena had garnered a large corner table at the back of the restaurant. Fresh flowers adorned the table in cut crystal vases. Flowing fountains lent an air of old European charm with richly appointed stone floors and Italian marble statues.

Nick made quick work of the introductions and helped Brooke to her seat. Rena asked to hold the baby immediately and the two women began a discussion about pregnancy and labor that left Nick and Tony to catch up on some business.

Joe and Ali arrived just as the wine was being served. Nick introduced Ali to Brooke and the three women conversed until their waiter arrived with menus. "The chef will prepare any special entrées you would like."

Nick asked Brooke if she wanted anything special. "I'm sure everything is wonderful. I'll order off the menu."

After they placed their orders, the women took turns holding Leah with looks of longing on their face and talked "baby" for twenty minutes. Finally Nick changed the subject. "Brooke's going to need a Web site for her bed-and-breakfast."

"I don't know what I'm doing really," she offered. "I'm going to start researching what I need beginning next week."

Ali grinned. "Are you kidding? Joe is a computer genius."

"Tell her like it is, Ali," Nick said with a grin. "He's a geek."

"He could probably whip you up a site in less than an hour," Ali said, looking at Joe with adoration.

Joe took her hand and winked at Brooke. "I don't walk on water, but I can help with that, if you'd like. Probably wouldn't take me very long once I had a clear picture of what you wanted."

"Really? That's...well, it's awfully nice of you but—"

"She accepts," Nick butted in, then shot Brooke a warning look. Hell, the woman had trouble accepting help, but there was no one better to get her started on her Web site than Joe.

Brooke shot him an angry glare then smiled at Joe. "Apparently, Nick doesn't think I can speak for myself."

"It's a trait of all the brothers," Rena said. "You'll get used to it. Just stick to your guns and they back down." She smiled sweetly at Tony, who seemed totally unfazed.

Nick sipped his wine and watched as Brooke interacted with his family. When the food came the women fought over who would hold Leah while Brooke ate her meal. It was only when Leah fussed, making frustrated baby noises that she was handed back to Brooke. From across the round table, he watched Brooke handle her child with care and patience. She had loving smiles for Leah even though the baby's complaints grew louder and louder. Finally, Brooke set down her fork and gave up on eating.

Nick stood and strode over to her. "Let me have her. I'm finished with my meal," he said, reaching for Leah. The baby's cries stopped and she lifted her arms to Nick. He picked her up and, having learned not to be stern with the baby's sensibilities, he said softly, "You gonna let your mama eat in peace now?"

Leah's cheeks plumped up, giving him a big smile.

"That's a girl."

Nick didn't miss Tony darting a quick knowing glance at Joe.

"Look at that," Rena said. "Nick's got a way with babies."

"I wouldn't have guessed," Ali said, in awe. "Looks good on you, Nick."

He took his seat as Leah laid her head on his chest and looked out toward the others. "She's a sweet kid, but children aren't in my future. Rena and Ali, it's up to you to carry on the Carlino name."

"We plan to," they said in unison then both laughed.

"Good, then you won't miss me when I'm gone. You'll have your own families."

Brooke's head shot up and all eyes at the table noticed her surprise.

"Of course, we'll miss you," Rena said, glancing from Brooke to Nick. "Where are you going?"

"If things go as planned, I'm leaving for Monte Carlo in a couple of months."

"For good?" Ali asked.

He nodded and when Leah squirmed, he rocked her in his arms to soothe her. "I'm itching to get back there."

"Nick?" Rena said, looking disappointed.

"I'm not going anywhere until your baby is born. And I'll be back for holidays. I'll be your kid's favorite uncle. Promise."

Joe shook his head. "I wouldn't plan ahead too far, bro."

Tony chimed in, glancing at the baby in his arms. "You never know what might happen."

"I'm going," Nick said adamantly. "As soon as we meet the terms of Santo's will."

Nick glanced at Brooke, sitting there, looking beautiful but wearing an unreadable expression. He had no idea what she was thinking. She seemed quieter than usual yet Rena and Ali took to her right away. Both Tony and Joe seemed to like her; Tony offering to help spread the word about her bed-and-breakfast and Joe setting up a date to design her website. Nick knew they had ulterior motives and were trying to trap him into losing the bet. Yet, watching Brooke interact with his family disturbed him on a number of levels, not the least of which being that she fit in so naturally.

Since Leah fell asleep shortly after the meal, they decided to order dessert at the restaurant rather than go back to the house. "Sorry," Brooke said, looking at Leah sleeping soundly in the infant seat, "but with a baby you have to be flexible."

"Oh, we understand," Ali said, "you'll just have to invite us over for coffee another day."

"Once I get my bed-and-breakfast going, I'll invite all of you over for dinner."

"Sounds good to me. Nick says you're a fantastic cook," Tony offered.

"Nick's been staying home nights," Joe added. "Can't say as I blame him."

Brooke blushed, her cheeks turning a bright shade of pink. "If that's a compliment, thank you. But just to make the record clear, Nick and I have a deal. He's been generous to me since the accident and I cook breakfast and dinner for him. But that's all I do for him." She glanced at Tony and Joe, and both men sat back in their seats.

"You tell them, Brooke," Ali said.

"I think we've been properly put in our place," Tony said with a grin. "Are we still invited for dinner?"

"Of course," Brooke said, her eyes going soft again. "I'd love to have you all as my guests."

"Great," Ali said. "I can't wait."

Coffee was served and a variety of desserts were put on the table; cannoli, tarimisu, almond pound cake, pastries and cookies. Nick sipped his coffee and leaned back. Every so often, he'd catch Brooke's eye and they'd share a look.

He wanted her and it was becoming increasingly harder to sleep under the same roof and not share a bed.

Something had to give.

Soon.

Brooke was pleased with the progress she'd made in just a few short weeks. Every day, she spent the morning weeding and planting flowers in her front yard as workmen painted the exterior of the house and a handyman did repairs to the bathrooms and bedrooms. She'd gone shopping for bed linens and fluffy bath towels and bought new curtains for the kitchen.

Joe had helped her with the website—they were now in the preliminary stages of the design. Ali had offered to take her shopping at her favorite out-of-the-way antique shops one day last week. They had a fun time, returning with some really beautiful items to decorate the rooms. Ali's friendship was both unexpected and welcome. By the end of the third week, Brooke felt her bed-and-breakfast would soon become a reality. Her dream was finally within her scopes.

She'd even heard from Molly Thornton, who finally returned her call to say she'd been out of town with her family for nearly a month and she'd been thrilled to hear from Brooke. Molly explained she was a schoolteacher now and had taken the summer off to do some traveling. She'd promised to stop by the house this afternoon.

Brooke had just finished feeding Leah in her new high chair, when a knock sounded at her door. Her daughter had graduated from a breast milk only diet to eating solid foods and managed to get half the jar of carrots anywhere but in her mouth. "Whoopsie!" she said to Leah, wiping clean her mouth and chin. "That'll be Molly. Can't have her meeting your carrot face, now."

There was additional pounding on the door, and Brooke called out, "Coming." She scooped Leah up in her arms. "You're going to like Molly. She's a nice lady."

Brooke opened the door wide, excited to see her friend again after so many years and her heart stopped for a moment, when instead of finding Molly, she came face to face with Dan Hartley, her ex.

A dozen questions entered her mind as her body began

to tremble. How had he found her? Why was he here? She noticed his eyes on Leah and hugged her tighter as she backed away.

He looked from her to the baby. "When were you going to tell me I had a daughter?"

"Dan, what are you doing here?"

"Don't you mean, how did I find you?"

She'd hoped she'd never have to lay eyes on him again. Though she knew she'd have to tell him about Leah soon, she wanted it to be on her own terms, once she'd thought things through, not unexpectedly like this. She didn't want Dan to have the upper hand, ever again.

"How could you do this to me, Brooke? I have a daughter and you don't tell me? You run away and hide her from me?"

"You didn't seem to mind taking off with your bimbo girlfriend, without a thought or care about me."

"You're not denying she's mine."

"I'm not having this conversation with you. I'm expecting someone to stop by at any moment. You want to talk to me, you call me on the phone."

"You want me to *call* you? I'm here to get to know my daughter, Brooke." His gaze roamed over Leah as if memorizing each little detail of her body. "She looks like you."

Leah turned away from him, nestling her face into Brooke's shoulders.

"Let me come inside. I want to see her."

No. No. No. Brooke wanted to scream. "You left us to have a child of your own, remember?"

Dan's expression changed to defiance. "I didn't know you were pregnant!"

"Would it have mattered? Sure didn't seem like it to me. You couldn't wait to pack up your things and get out.

You had something better waiting for you—the woman you really loved and the baby you were having with her. So, why don't you go back to your *something better.*"

He winced as his brown eyes went dark. "She lost the baby. Things didn't work out between us."

Brooke's anger rose and her sense of betrayal intensified. Her entire body shook. "So now you want to get to know Leah? So now you want to impose on our lives? I'm sorry for the loss of the child, but that doesn't excuse your behavior. And I'm going to tell you this *just once,* Leah isn't anybody's second choice. Would we even be having this conversation if things had worked out? Would you even care about the child you abandoned?"

"Hell, Brooke, be reasonable. I didn't know you were going to have my child."

"That might be true, but you were having an affair behind my back and you managed to get another woman pregnant while you were married to me."

"I know. I made a mistake."

"You slept with both of us at the same time. That makes you a snake in my book. I don't want you anywhere near Leah, ever."

"You're hurt and angry."

"Damn right I am. But I'm over you and moving on with my life. I want you off my porch right now. If you want to talk to me, call me. You're not coming into my home."

With that, Brooke slammed the door in his face and bolted it shut.

She waited and it was several minutes before she heard him get into his car and pull away. She stood there shaking and wishing this were all a bad dream. She had trouble fusing her thoughts together, trying to make sense of what just happened. She still didn't know how he'd found out about Leah or how he knew how to find her.

Thankfully, Leah went down for her nap without a fuss and she'd just walked out of the downstairs bedroom when another knock came at her door. She nearly jumped out of her skin. She moved to the parlor window, carefully parted the sheer draperies and peered out. Relief seeped in when she saw a woman on her porch.

Brooke opened the door and found Molly's smiling face. She hadn't changed much over the years. Her hair was a darker shade of auburn and she wore it shorter in a stylish cut. "It's good to see you, Brooke. You look exactly the same."

"Molly, come in," she said, trying to hold it together. "It's good to see you, too." A friendly face was exactly what she needed at the moment.

They fell into a heartwarming embrace.

Then Brooke broke down and cried.

Seven

Brooke entered the Carlino home a little later than usual that afternoon, her routine disrupted by seeing her ex and the implications that involved. Thankfully, Molly had been as sweet as ever and lent an ear to her troubles. Just having someone listen, just being able to open up to a friend, made her situation seem more than hopeless. They'd spent the better part of the afternoon talking and catching up. Brooke hadn't had this type of outlet in a long time and it felt good. She had her mother to talk to, but her mother had had enough grief in her life and had finally found happiness. The last thing Brooke wanted to do was burden her with her troubles. So Molly's timing today had been perfect. Brooke didn't know how she would have made it through the day without her.

Now, at the Carlino house without Molly's strong shoulder to lean on, Brooke's fears returned and a knot twisted in her stomach. All she could think about was seeing Dan's angry face. What would he do? She'd literally kicked him off her property and she knew he wouldn't let it go. He'd be back. Deep in thought and worried to death, she cooked the meal quickly and didn't say much to Nick all throughout dinner. She couldn't eat a thing and he asked her three times if anything was wrong, but she denied there was and rushed out of the kitchen and away from him as soon as she could.

Of all nights for Leah to go to sleep early, tonight wasn't the night. Brooke wanted to hold her and play their silly little games and read her a story, keeping her close and feeding off the love they had for each other. Instead, she sat on her bed and watched Leah sleep, worried about her future. When Brooke laid her head down and tried to sleep, old haunting feelings of betrayal, of not being good enough for Dan, of hating him and what he'd done to her, came rushing forth. Her thoughts wouldn't go away, they wouldn't give her peace.

Tears streamed down her face, as Molly's words came back to her. "You've come so far, Brooke." And she had. She wasn't the wilting wallflower from the wrong side of the tracks anymore. It wasn't her, but Dan, who'd done wrong. She shouldn't be torturing herself like this. She deserved better. She deserved more.

She heard footsteps going down the hallway and Nick's bedroom door closing shut.

She was through denying that *the more* she wanted was Nick.

He'd given her an open invitation to join him in bed.

He was the balm she needed to soothe her restlessness.

And why not? They were two consenting adults and he'd made it clear that he wanted her with no strings attached. Her life was complicated enough—she didn't want strings either. He was leaving the country soon and that would ensure no complications.

"He's just down the hall," she whispered into the darkness and rose from the bed. She dressed in a sheer white summer nightie, checked on Leah, who was still sound asleep and tiptoed downstairs. Her bravado needed a little help. She grabbed a bottle of fine Carlino merlot and two goblets and went back up.

Behind Nick's door, she heard the television. She knocked and didn't bother to wait for him to answer. She slowly pushed open the door.

Nick gazed at her from his bed. He clicked off the TV. "Brooke, is something wrong?"

This was Nick Carlino, the boy she'd once loved, the boy she had wanted to claim her virginity. It was too late for that, but she'd never stopped wondering about Nick. She'd dreamt about this moment so many times through the years that she had trouble believing she was actually standing here, offering herself to him. "You said sex can be simple."

Nick peered at her with assessing eyes, his gaze flowing over her lacy white gown that bared more cleavage and leg than she'd ever let him see before.

He stood up. "It can be."

He looked like sex personified in a pair of jeans and nothing else. His body tight and muscled, his skin a golden bronze. Brooke wondered how she'd been able to stay away from him so long.

"I need simple, Nick. With you."

He walked over to her and took the wine bottle from her hand. "You want to tell me what changed your mind?"

She closed her eyes. "No."

"You really want wine right now?"

"No."

He set the wine bottle down and then the glasses. "I've been waiting for you," he said softly, then took her into his arms, bringing her in close. Their bodies meshed perfectly and she ran her fingers across his chest, stroking him before he had a chance to kiss her. She heard his intake of breath.

"It's a long time coming, honey." Then he bent his head and brushed his lips to hers gently, teasing, stroking her lips with his tongue until she whimpered his name.

His kiss went deeper and deeper until they simultaneously mated tongues, the potent sensation sweeping them both up into a hot raging storm of desire. Nick cupped her neck and angled her head to take her fully then he wove his fingers into her hair and muttered quiet oaths between kisses that only spurred her passion further.

He moved his lips lower, to her throat and down her shoulders, planting moist delicious kisses there, his hands riding up and down her sides. She arched for him and he didn't bother getting tangled up in her nightgown, he removed it with one quick yank of the spaghetti straps down her shoulders. The garment slowly dropped down her legs to the floor.

Her breasts sprung out—now her tiny white thong was all that was left on her body. Nick's gaze filled with lust and admiration. "No more mommy clothes."

Throaty laughter spilled out. "Not tonight."

Nick cupped her breasts and stroked with nimble fingers, driving her completely insane. He whispered, "I don't care what you say, those clothes are still a turn-on."

"Are you saying I turn you on, night and day?"

"Pretty much." He bent his head and kissed one breast, then the other. "Whatever brought you here, I'm damn glad." He cupped her behind and pressed her belly to his erection.

"I see how glad you are."

He groaned when she rubbed harder against him.

"Don't tease me, Brooke."

"Why," she said breathlessly. "What will you do?"

He grinned wickedly then picked her up and lifted her until she was over the bed. "This." He dropped her a few inches and she bounced once, before settling in. He didn't give her time to react, joining her on the bed, covering her with his body.

"You feel good."

The heat of his gaze and the hungry look in his eyes told her playtime was over. Her throat constricted and she managed, "So do you, Nick."

She wove her hands into his hair, threading her fingers through the dark locks, gazing into his eyes, then lifted up to brush a quick kiss to his lips. He lowered her down and pinned her hands above her head, then proceeded to make love to her body with his mouth. She was trapped by his hold, but more by the way he touched and caressed every inch of her. Little moans escaped her throat as she closed off her mind to everything but the pleasure Nick gave her.

Nick released her hands then lowered himself down on the bed, and kneeled before her. He lifted her legs and pressed his hand to her core, the heat of his palm creating hot moist tingles of excitement. He rubbed his palm over her several times then angled his head and brought his mouth to her.

She arched and gave him access, feeling every kiss, every stroke of his tongue in her most sensitized spot. The pleasure was exquisite and torturous and Brooke thrashed her head back and forth, absorbing the sensations whipping through her.

Pressure built quickly and she panted out breaths, the tension almost too much to bear.

Nick released her then and lay beside her, unsnapping his jeans. "Let me," she whispered, turning toward him and lowering his zipper. She helped him out of his jeans and then took his manhood in her hands, stroking him lightly.

"You're wicked cruel," Nick said with a smile.

"You're welcome."

He lay back, taking heavy breaths as she continued to stroke him, his erection thick in her hands. She felt so free and open with Nick, the final culmination of years of wondering and dreaming about this night that she wouldn't hold back.

Tonight was all about sex and she couldn't think of a better partner than deadly handsome, dangerous Nick Carlino.

Brooke could be dangerous too and she was about to show him how much. She slid her hand up and down his length, enjoying the contrast of hard muscle against silken skin. He grew harder in her hands and when she rubbed her finger over the tip, a guttural groan emanated from his throat.

A slim path of moonlight streamed into the room casting shadows on his perfect body. "I want you on top," he demanded, his gaze burning hot.

She gulped oxygen and waited while he took care of protection. Then he lifted her over him and she straddled his legs, her back arching slightly.

"Do you have any idea how beautiful you look right now?"

A charmer and a sweet-talker, Brooke often didn't take Nick seriously, but there was a rich sincere tone to his voice now and even though she didn't think her body was beautiful, not after stretch marks and breasts that had lost their ripeness, she peered into his half-lidded, sex-hazy eyes and saw that he believed it.

He took her hips in his big hands and guided her down. She felt the initial touch of his penis and a dam of desire broke as her body opened for him. She lowered down a little more, taking him in slowly, deliberately, absorbing the feel of him inside her.

She closed her eyes to feel the height of every sensation. It was sheer heaven. She'd gone so long without this natural act. At this time in her life, she needed Nick and the sexual satisfaction he could provide for her.

Nick moved his hips and thrust into her, testing her and tempting her to take all of him. She complied easily, her body moist and ready to accommodate his needs. She sunk down deeper and through the dim light, she witnessed his expression change. He whispered words of encouragement as she moved on him, up and down, each intense thrust bringing her closer to the brink of fulfillment.

Nick lifted up and wrapped his arms around her, holding her tight as she moved on him. He cupped her derriere and brought his mouth to hers, slanting fiery hot kisses over her lips. She was ready, so ready.

"Together," he said, between kisses. "We're doing this together."

Brooke understood and when Nick rolled her onto her back, she accommodated his full weight. He adjusted his position and took control. He fondled her breasts as he kissed her, driving her nearly insane. His thrusts were powerful and deliberate, each one meant to arouse and tease until she couldn't hold back her release. Her breaths came fast and hard. Nick was relentless, his body covering hers. She held him around the neck as he drove his thrusts home.

Hot waves swirled and electric jolts coursed through her body. She cried out with little moans, her face contorting as she took on the extreme, heady pleasure. Their release erupted, shattered and consumed. Just as he'd promised, they came at the same time and the notion left her with a breathless smile.

Nick lowered his body down and she breathed in the scent of man and musk and sex. He stroked her face gently and kissed her again before moving off her to roll onto his back. "That might have been worth the wait."

Brooke chuckled. "It's only been a few weeks."

Nick moved onto his side and with a finger to her chin turned her face to his. "More like thirteen years."

Her throat tightened and she tried to make light of it. "Ancient history."

"I wanted you back then, Brooke. I know you don't believe it, but it's true."

Brooke didn't believe it. "Let's not talk about the past."

Nick bent his head to kiss her lightly. "Okay, let's talk about how amazing you are."

The compliment made her uneasy. "I bet you say that to all the girls."

Nick remained silent and Brooke realized that she had really stepped into it now. Her obvious attempt at humor failed.

"Listen," Nick said in a serious tone, "I don't sleep with a different woman every night. That's never been my style. I actually have to like the woman and respect her, before I take her to bed."

"Okay," Brooke said, oddly believing him. He was a man with integrity.

"What happened between us just now was amazing."

Brooke agreed with a nod. "For me, it was."

Nick took her into his arms and laid her head on his chest. "For me too."

She could stay in his arms all night, but thought better of it. "I'd better check on Leah."

She found her nightie and tossed it over her head then made a move to go, but Nick stopped her, taking her hand. "Come back."

"I, uh, we're still keeping this simple, right?"

"Simple," Nick agreed without hesitation, releasing her from his grasp.

"Okay, then I'll be back."

Nick put on his boxers and got out of bed to pour two glasses of wine. He didn't know what brought Brooke to him tonight and he wasn't going to look a gift horse in the mouth. But he couldn't help wondering. She'd been bold and vulnerable at the same time, but it was the underlying trepidation in her eyes that she'd tried to hide that bothered him. Something was up with her—something had changed to bring her to his bed. Maybe he shouldn't want to know and maybe he was better off not knowing but the hell of it was, he did want to know.

Sex with her was better than he'd imagined. And he'd done a lot of imagining over the years. Whenever he was at his lowest points in life, he'd think about Brooke Hamilton and her image would make him smile. But at the same time, it would leave him empty.

He'd done the right thing back then, but it was different now and Brooke seemed to want what he did. Simple and uncomplicated. Two words Nick knew a lot about when it came to women.

He set the bottle down, the Carlino Wines label facing him, a constant reminder of the sacrifices forced down his throat for the sake of the company. He wanted out. He wanted away from here and the sooner the better. His old man wouldn't win. Not ultimately. Nick would win his bet with his brothers and that would be that.

When Brooke reappeared in his doorway, he was swept up by the look in her stunning blue-green eyes. It was a turn-on just seeing her framed by the moonlight, her blond hair tousled and the strap of her nightie falling down her shoulder.

"Hi," she whispered.

"How's Leah?"

She smiled. "Sleeping like an angel."

Nick walked over to her and took her hand. "Come back to bed."

She hesitated and peered at him with eyes that seemed haunted. "This isn't a mistake, is it?"

Nick put his hands on her shoulders and caressed her lightly. Touching her spurred something fierce within him and he followed the path of her slender body, his hands roaming down her sides until he reached her waist. He pulled her close and she squeezed her eyes shut.

"Doesn't feel like a mistake." He brushed a kiss to her lips. "Does it to you?"

She shook her head and those gorgeous eyes caught him in a spell. "No, but it's just that I…"

"Just that you, what?"

"Nothing, Nick." She pulled away from him to pick up the two goblets of wine. She handed him one, then took a sip of her own, her demeanor changing. "I haven't been able to drink wine or anything alcoholic in a while. This tastes delicious."

Nick blinked and wondered about her sudden mood change but not enough to destroy the evening. He had a beautiful woman in his room, drinking wine after a wicked time between the sheets and he wanted her back in his bed. He wasn't through with Brooke Hamilton yet.

She took a few more sips then set the glass on the nightstand. Nick polished his merlot off easily, then sat down on the bed and grabbed her hand. With a tug, he pulled her onto his lap. She fell onto him gracefully and wrapped her arms around his neck.

He nibbled on her throat and his voice took on a low rich rasp. "I want to make love to you all night long."

"That's why I'm here," she answered softly.

Nick's questions were quelled with her response. He gave up trying to figure her out and simply enjoyed the fact she was so willing. He lifted her off him and laid her down on the bed. She reached for him with outstretched arms causing his heart to hammer and his body to tighten instantly.

He made love to her slowly this time, peeling away her clothes and relishing each morsel of her body. He took care and time and enjoyed her as he'd never enjoyed another woman. She was hot and sexy and fun and feisty in bed. She gave as much as she took and as the night wore on, they made love again and again.

Each time was different and better than the last. Nick hadn't had sex like this in a long time. It was almost as if Brooke had been dying of thirst and once she was offered a drink she couldn't get enough. Lucky for him.

Sometime during the late night, Brooke must have tiptoed out of bed, because Nick woke up alone. Oddly, the sense of loss he experienced when he found her gone puzzled him. They'd certainly had a satisfying night between the sheets and it wasn't unusual for him to wake up alone after being with a woman. Usually, he preferred it that way.

Nick showered and dressed and made his way down the hallway. He knocked on Brooke's door softly, and when no one answered, he opened it to find both mother and baby weren't there.

He strode downstairs and found them in the kitchen.

Brooke stood at the kitchen counter feeding Leah her breakfast. The little girl was outgrowing her infant seat quickly. Brooke was so intent on spooning squash into her mouth, she didn't notice him enter the room. He walked up behind her and wrapped his arms around her waist. "Morning," he said. When she turned around, he planted a kiss to her lips.

"Morning," she said, taking only a second to look at him before turning back to her daughter. "Watch out, Leah's in a squash-tossing mood this morning."

Nick patted Leah's head, her loose little blond curls bouncy under his palm. "You need a high chair, kid. I'll order one and have it delivered today."

Brooke put Leah's spoon down and stared at him. "Nick, you will not."

"Why not? She's outgrowing that seat she's in."

"Because for one, she has a high chair at my house, and for two, we'll be moving out in a few weeks. We can make do until then."

"Hey, did you get up on the wrong side of the bed?"

Brooke's defiant expression changed to something more reasonable. "No, I didn't." Then a little smile emerged and she softened her tone. "I got up feeling pretty wonderful this morning."

"You can thank me for that later." He grabbed a cup by the coffeemaker and poured his coffee.

"I thought I showed my appreciation last night."

Nick chuckled and was glad feisty Brooke was back. They drove each other crazy last night, a memory that would stay with him long after she was gone. He sipped his coffee. "What are you doing tonight after work?"

"Cooking for you and then falling into bed. I didn't get a whole lot of sleep last night. Why?"

He shrugged. The thought just popped into his head.

"There's a new pizza place in town and I hear it's pretty good. I thought you'd like to try it. Nothing fancy, sawdust on the floor."

The incredible hue in her eyes softened and just when he thought she'd agree, she turned her attention away and shook her head. "I don't think so."

"We'll take Leah."

"It's not that. I just don't think it's a good idea."

"Pizza is always a good idea."

She wiped her daughter's chin then the rest of her face and removed her from the infant seat. With Leah on her hip, she turned to him. That underlying worry he'd seen last night reappeared. "I've got a lot going on right now, Nick. I...can't."

"What's going on?"

"Nothing." She clammed up and again he wished she'd tell him what had put that wary look on her face. "We're keeping this simple and I really need that right now."

"It's what we agreed on. I'm a man of my word."

She sighed deeply. "Your breakfast is on the stove. I'm not hungry this morning."

Hell.

"Don't cook tonight. I'll bring pizza home."

She turned away from him and busied herself with dishing up his meal. "Okay. If that's what you feel like having tonight. It's fine with me."

Nick spent the morning at the Carlino offices in town. More than once he thought about Brooke and that haunted look on her face. He told himself to butt out, that *simple* meant not getting involved too personally. Leah's face popped into his head and he figured Brooke's worry might have something to do with her baby. If that were the case, she might need his help. But Leah looked like the picture of health. He didn't know much about kids but he knew that Leah was a happy child.

Brooke was a fantastic mother.

After lunch, Nick found himself in front of Brooke's bed-and-breakfast. He had no reason to stop by other than he couldn't stop thinking about her. He got out of his car and the first thing he noticed was how manicured the front lawn appeared. New grass grew along the walkway leading up to the front door. A garden of yellow, pink and lavender flowers sprouted from the borders on either side of the front porch. The exterior walls of the house were painted with a fresh coat of yellow paint and half of the shutters were gleaming white, the other half layered with primer.

Nick knocked on the door. When Brooke didn't answer, he knocked again, louder. He saw her part curtains in a big box window and glance first at his SUV, then gaze at him. The look of pure relief on her face gave him pause.

A second later, the door opened and he grinned, seeing the splotches of cornflower blue paint on her nose and chin. Her oversized T-shirt and denim jeans were splashed with streaks of paint in various colors. In the background, he heard Leah's cries of complaint. "Did you get any paint *on* the walls?"

"Funny, Nick," she said, heaving a big sigh and opening the door wider to allow him entrance. "Come in."

As she waited for him to step inside, he noticed her scanning the street before shutting the door and bolting it. "I'm painting one of the bedrooms and Leah's not happy about it." She headed toward the sound of Leah's cries.

Nick followed her past the parlor and up the staircase. "I don't want her inhaling the fumes, so she's complaining about being out in the hallway."

Once he reached the hallway, the baby gave him a big smile from inside her playpen and lifted her arms out toward him. He bent to lift her up and Leah tucked her little body against him. Nick stroked her soft curls as her baby scent wafted to his nostrils.

Brooke looked at the two of them together and her lips pulled down in a frown. "What are you doing here?"

Was this the same woman who'd been sweet, sexy and loving in his arms last night? Brooke seemed to be out of sorts and jumpy as if she'd lose it at any second. It was exactly why he'd come here today. Something was wrong and she wouldn't confide in him. The truth was, he was worried about them though he wouldn't say it out loud. "I had an appointment with a client. It was on my way and I thought I'd stop in and see your progress. The outside is taking shape."

"Thanks. It's slow going today though. Leah's not cooperating."

"She's fine now." He couldn't help it if the kid liked him, could he?

The furniture was in the middle of the room covered with a big drop cloth. Brooke must have dragged it there and covered it without any help. Hell, he could have a crew of painters out here tomorrow and every room painted to her specifications if she'd allow him. But he wouldn't even suggest it. She budgeted for the exterior to be professionally painted and took on the interior work herself. He had to admire her work ethic and pride. He knew she loved working on this place. *That* was not what was making her edgy.

"She'll be worse once you're gone."

"Then I won't leave."

Brooke glanced at him. "You've got better things to do."

Leah bumped her head against his chin and he flinched

from the hard knock that gnashed his teeth together. He ground out, "Can't think of anything."

Brooke shook her head and laughed. "She's got you conned, Nick."

"I'll help you paint. We can take turns with her."

Brooke scoffed and the look on her face annoyed him. "You're dressed like a million bucks."

"I'll take off my clothes. Anything to accommodate a lady."

"Thanks, but no thanks."

"I'm serious, Brooke. I have a free afternoon. I've got an old pair of sweats in my car."

Before she could answer, her cell phone rang. Nick glanced at it vibrating on the window ledge. One ring. Two rings. Brooke's eyes went wide but she didn't make a move to answer it.

"Want me to hand it to you?" he asked.

"No! Don't get it." Brooke's face froze with fear. She glanced at the phone as if it were death warmed over. "I'm not going to answer." When the phone stopped ringing, her body slumped and she let her breath out.

Nick set Leah down in her playpen and strode over to Brooke. "What the hell's wrong? The phone scared the crap outta you."

"Nothing's wrong." She tried to smooth over her fear by softening her tone, but Nick saw straight through that. "I can't talk right now. I have to finish painting, that's all."

"And you don't want to know who it was?"

"It was Molly," she said without skipping a beat. "You remember Molly Thornton, don't you? She's teaching school now and I told her to call, but I'm too busy to talk. You know how women are, once they get on the phone, they don't stop. I'm really eager to finish this room today."

Nick narrowed his eyes. "You're a terrible liar."

Brooke squeezed her eyes shut. He watched turmoil cross her features. When she opened her eyes to him, she hoisted her chin, her stubborn face on. "Are you going to help me paint this room or what?"

"Yeah, I'll help," he said, angry that she'd lied to him. Why the hell he cared baffled him. She wanted simple and so did he.

He walked out to his car and got his sweats. He couldn't remember the last time he'd picked up a paintbrush.

If ever.

Eight

Nick was true to his word. He helped her paint the bedroom and they took turns with Leah when she fussed. It was a sight, seeing Nick with paint smudging his usually impeccably groomed face. Half an hour into it, his sweats were in no better shape than her clothes. She kept fixating on the speck of blue paint on Nick's eyelid whenever they spoke to keep from thinking about the *call*. She suspected it was Dan but she hadn't listened to her voicemail. It could have been Molly leaving her a message. Wishful thinking, she supposed because from the look on Dan's face yesterday, she didn't think he would give up. Oddly, having Nick with her today calmed her nerves.

By six o'clock they'd finished the room. Both stood back to admire their work. "Looks nice, a soft shade of blue and once I get the furniture back in place, I can call this room ready to rent. Only three more to go."

It was a good thing too, because the money she'd saved

for repairs and renovation, meager as it was, had been stretched to its limit.

"I'll call for pizza and once the paint dries, we'll put the furniture back."

Brooke had a protest on her lips, but Nick had turned his back on her, his cell in hand making the call. "What kind do you want?"

"Vegetarian."

He winced and ordered two pizzas, one with veggies and one fully loaded. "They'll be here in thirty minutes," he said. "Where can I clean up? I need a shower."

"Oh." That caught her off guard. Images of Nick naked in the shower made her mind sizzle with promising thoughts. Making love to him last night had been better than any of her wild imaginings.

Nick grinned as if reading her mind and approached her. "You could use one too."

The dimples of doom emerged on his face in a way that beckoned and brought even more lusty thoughts. After a full day of being shuffled back and forth, played with and read to, Leah had conked out. Her naps usually lasted at least an hour, so Brooke couldn't use her for an excuse.

Not that she wanted one.

Nick came within a breath of her and their eyes met. Once again, she focused on that blue fleck of paint on his eyelid and inhaled sharply. He dipped his finger onto his wet paintbrush coming up with a dollop of cornflower blue and spread it across her throat in a slow caress. "You're gonna need a good scrubbing to get all that paint off." His brows lifted, then he bent his head and brushed a lingering kiss to her lips.

Brooke trembled and her eyes fluttered closed. Every nerve in her body tightened. She couldn't refuse Nick and the promise of pleasure he would give to her. For a few minutes, he could take her away from her troubles and make her forget.

It was simple sex, she reminded herself. She took his hand and led him to the upstairs shower in the corner room. "It's small. We'll have to squeeze in together."

"I like the way you think." Nick lifted his sweatshirt over his head and tossed it in the corner. With his muscled chest bare, she itched to touch every inch of taut skin then devour him with her mouth.

He skimmed the edge of her shirt, pushing it up and over her head, exposing her white cotton bra. His dimples popped out and an appreciative smile spread across his face. "You've changed my opinion of soccer moms."

Brooke swatted at him, but he grabbed her wrist and wound her arm around his neck. He pressed his lips to hers in a more demanding kiss, one that had them pushing and tugging off the rest of their clothes. Nick pulled her into the shower stall, turned the water on to a hot steamy spray then backed her up against the tiled wall.

He was beautiful and sleek and tan, built like a superior athlete and at the moment, he was all hers.

They didn't even try to scrub each other, but allowed the steam to do that job while they kissed and touched and played in the shower. Brooke devoured him with her mouth as she'd planned and he, in turn, did the same. His hands slid all over her—pausing in her most erotic spots long enough to drive her completely crazy.

Nick had expert hands and a mouth that was made for pleasure. He brought her to the brink of climax with just a few exquisite touches to her inner folds, then he bent down and took her into his mouth. She grabbed his hair in her hands when she no longer could hold on and the rush of raining waters drowned out her little cries of ecstasy as her body convulsed.

She lay back against the tile, her gaze hazy and her body sated. Nick smiled at her. "I like that look on you."

"Feels pretty good too."

Nick kissed her again and his massive erection rubbed her belly. She reached down and took him into her hands, smiling when his face grew taut and his eyes closed with pleasure. "Wicked cruel."

"That's me," she said, sliding him through her fingers, his shaft growing even larger. He only allowed a minute of stroking before he stopped her. "No more," he said then lifted her up in his arms and wrapped her legs around his waist. He kissed her hard, stroking her with his tongue, then plunged deep into her moist body, his hands on her waist guiding her movements.

She arched back and he thrust harder and harder. "Brooke," he muttered, his voice deep and primal. His release came shortly after, in hard bursts of power that stirred her to another amazing climax. Her body shuddered for several long seconds and then she went limp in his arms. He held her that way for a long time after he shut the water off.

Nick made her forget her troubles for a short time and gave her more pleasure than any man she'd known. She was grateful to him for that, but reality knocked her hard when Dan's angry face stole into her mind. It was like a splash of freezing cold water on her sated body. "I'd better check on Leah," she said hastily. "And the pizza will be delivered soon." She left Nick standing there, gloriously naked with a puzzled look on his face.

"She's cutting her first tooth," Brooke said to Molly on the phone much later that night in her bedroom. Leah had fussed all evening long requiring all of Brooke's attention.

"I can see the first buds coming through her gums. No wonder she's been out of sorts."

"Oh, I remember that phase. Sometimes they wake up with teeth in their mouth and sometimes it's a major trauma when a tooth comes in." Molly had two children, a six-year-old boy and a four-year-old girl.

"I think Leah is somewhere in between. She's really such a good baby most of the time, but I know her little gums are bothering her."

"Teething rings work well," Molly said. "Do you have one?"

"Yes and she likes it. She gnawed on it until she finally fell asleep." It was ten o'clock, late for Leah to fall asleep. But between a late nap and the teething, it had taken a long time for Brooke to get her down.

That late nap allowed Brooke time alone with Nick, always a risky proposition. He was her guilty pleasure and as long as she thought about him that way, she'd manage okay. No hearth and home thoughts of Nick, she warned herself.

"Brooke, what happened with your ex? Did you hear from him today?" Molly asked, more than mildly curious.

"He called, but I didn't pick up the phone. The voicemail was not pretty. I don't know what to do. He's so angry with me but at the same time, there's an undertone of civility. I think he wants a second chance, for Leah's sake."

"He told you that on the voicemail?"

"It's the impression I got."

"And how do you feel about that? Would you ever take him back?"

"No. Never. I'm not in love with him. He killed that a long time ago. He's Leah's father and I'm going to have to deal with that sooner or later. I'm just so scared."

"Well, you're not alone. I'm here if you need me."

"I know, Molly. Thank you." But it was Nick's image that popped into her mind whenever the fear got to her. She slammed her eyes shut to block him out. She didn't want to rely on him. She wouldn't allow herself to feel anything for him. He was a walking heartbreak and she'd be a fool to fall for him. Yet, she knew in her heart, he'd be there for her, if she really needed him. That's why she wouldn't confide in him about Dan. She couldn't afford the luxury of getting that close to him. She had to be strong and independent. She'd never place her trust in another man ever again. "You've always been a good friend. I'm sorry we can't meet for lunch tomorrow. I don't know how fussy Leah will be."

"That's okay. We'll do it another time. Remember, I'm here if you need me."

"I know and I'll call you soon, I promise."

Brooke hung up the phone and walked over to Leah's little bed. Her baby looked peaceful, sleeping soundly. Instead of undressing, Brooke had something on her mind, something that had occurred to her after two slices of pizza and a beer tonight, in the aftermath of making love with Nick. But this was the first chance she'd had to address it.

She left her room, keeping the door open in case Leah woke, then strode down the hall to Nick's bedroom. She knocked and waited.

He opened the door with his cell phone to his ear and gestured for her to come in. She thought she heard a woman's voice on the other end of the phone and immediately her jaw clenched. A sense of dread coursed through her system and raw jealousy emerged. It hit her hard and she denied it over and over in her mind.

Nick could do whatever he wanted.

She had no hold on him.

Was he making a date with another woman?

He'd told her he didn't see more than one woman at a time. Had he lied? She fought her trust issues, reminding herself that she and Nick had an uncomplicated relationship. Still, her ego would be trampled if Nick were seeing someone else.

"Hi. That was Rena," he said to her, looking thoughtful after the call ended. "She couldn't sleep and needed to talk. Tony's out cold."

"So, you're her sounding board," she asked, ridiculously relieved he'd been speaking with his sister-in-law.

His grin spread wide and stole her breath. "Yeah, I'm willing to listen to complaints about my brothers anytime."

"She was complaining?"

"Venting. Tony's been hovering and protective. She's due in just a week or two."

"It's an emotional time," Brooke offered. "I remember my mood swings were like a roller-coaster ride, up and down, mostly down."

It was ironic that the subject led to this, because that's exactly why she'd come to his room tonight.

"Yeah, that sounds like Rena too."

He glanced at her, as if finally realizing she was there. He focused on her mouth, arched a brow and waited.

Suddenly, Brooke's throat constricted. She'd thought it would so easy to bring this up, but now found herself unbelievably speechless. "I, uh, about this afternoon."

"The best shower I've ever had."

"Nick," she said, glad he was the one to mention it. "We didn't use any protection."

Nick studied her a moment, his gaze roaming from her eyes to her nose, to her mouth and lower still, taking his time. When he lifted his gaze back to hers, once again he appeared thoughtful. "I'm healthy, Brooke. I'd never endanger you."

"Okay." She took a big swallow and nodded. "But it's more than—"

"If you're worried about getting pregnant, don't. I can't have children."

That came out of the blue and was so unexpected, her mouth dropped open in surprise. "You…can't?"

He shook his head. "No, but it was my choice."

"What do you mean, it was your choice?"

Nick took her hand and led her to the bed. He sat down and pulled her next to him. His fingers laced with hers and he let out a heavy sigh. "About five years ago my father pissed me off, as usual. That wasn't new, but I was so angry with him I wanted to do something that would show him he couldn't control me any longer. I fixed that part of my anatomy so I couldn't give him an heir."

"Wow," Brooke said, her brows furrowing together. "You must have really wanted—"

"I wanted to hurt him. It was wrong, but a cocky twenty-something, and my rage at my father made me do some crazy things."

"Oh Nick. I'm sorry. You must regret that."

Nick squeezed her hand. "I don't. I'm not father material. I knew I'd never make a good father. I wasn't lying when I said I'd be happy being the favorite uncle. Joe and Tony will take care of the baby-making in the family."

Brooke felt like crying for Nick. Imagine that, the sexy dangerous and wealthy wine magnate had Brooke's sympathy. "What did your father do when he found out?"

"The hell of it was I never told him. My brothers talked me out of it and I wasn't sure that was the right move, but they convinced me. Now that he's gone, I'm glad I didn't, so I owe my brothers for that."

"Nick, what did he do to make you hate him so much. Was he…abusive?"

Nick smiled with sadness darkening his eyes. "No, never. But he was ruthless when he wanted something. He destroyed my career."

Brooke remembered Nick had told her a few times, he didn't have everything he wanted. Searching her memory, she recalled his one passion. The one thing that he'd wanted above all else. "Baseball?"

He put his head down and dragged her hand to his lap, holding tight. "I was just a kid with a dream." Deep emotion weighted his words. "I was good, Brooke."

"I remember."

"I'd made the minor leagues and was on my way to the majors, but dear old dad wanted his boys to run the wine business. He wanted us to love his legacy as much as he did. None of us did. I was his last chance."

Nick went on to tell the details of the incidents that crushed his baseball career. The lies, the deception and the manipulations. He spoke about Candy Rae and Brooke's spine stiffened when she learned about her part in the deception. Nick had been just a young boy with his whole life ahead of him. How devastating for him to go through that, knowing his father disregarded his wishes to manipulate him into a life he didn't want. Brooke finally understood why Nick wanted nothing to do with the company. It signified all he'd lost.

"Then I had my accident during the game. I know in my head my father didn't physically injure me so I couldn't play again, but he sure as hell put pressure on me and had me rattled enough to make a fool move on the field. I was recovering from the surgery too, but before I knew what happened, the team released me. I know my father had something to do with that."

Brooke had heard rumors about Santo Carlino when she'd lived in Napa as a young girl. He'd been a powerful and ruthless businessman. "I'm sorry."

"Don't be. I'm only telling you this to ease your mind about being with me."

"Is that the only reason, Nick?" She shouldn't have asked. She never knew when to keep her trap shut.

He turned to face her, his gaze piercing hers. "It's been a long time since I've spoken about this. And only to my brothers. I guess I figured you'd understand."

"I do." She smiled and stroked his cheek gently, his day old stubble rough under her palm. "But I'm sorry for more than what you've gone through. I'm sorry for thinking having money and good looks meant you had everything you wanted."

"You like my looks?" he said, in an attempt to lighten the mood.

"Yes, I like your looks," she said, not taking the bait to banter. This was serious and she wouldn't let Nick make light of it. "I've misjudged you and I apologize."

He brought her hand to his mouth and gently kissed the inner skin of her palm. "Thanks."

They sat in the dark, holding hands, the intimacy of the moment more profound than the sex they'd experienced these past few days. Brooke's heart ached for him in a way she'd never be able to justify or explain to another person.

Because this was Nick.

And she was falling in love with him.

"Stupid, stupid, stupid," Brooke muttered, as she gave the dining room table a second polish, the cloth in her hand circling faster and faster, to match the crazy beating of her heart. "How could Mommy do that? How could she fall in love with Nick again?" she asked Leah, who played with a Baby Elmo music box on the floor. Leah looked up with a questioning pout on her little lips. To add insult to injury, her daughter's eyes rounded and searched the room at the mere mention of Nick's name. Even her child was smitten with him.

Her life was in shambles and she didn't have a solution to either of her dilemmas.

Dan wanted to know his daughter and start over, and Nick, the man she loved, wanted to be rid of Napa in the worst way. One man was coming back into her life, another leaving for good. And it was all wrong.

When her cell phone rang, Brooke didn't jump and she didn't panic. It was time for her to come to terms with her life and fix what she could. She noted Dan's number on the screen and took a deep breath before answering. "Hello."

"It's Dan, honey."

Honey?

"I'm only in Napa for a few more days. I'd like to come see you. We have things to talk about. Things to work out. I know I made a mistake leaving you."

"Yes, you did, Dan. But that's over now."

"It doesn't have to be. I want to talk to you, Brooke."

There was a calm and amenable tone to his voice today, but she still didn't trust it, or him. "I suppose we do have things to talk about."

"Can I come over?"

"Today's not good, Dan. Come tomorrow afternoon. We'll talk."

After Brooke hung up the phone, she slumped down in a chair and put her head in her hands. She couldn't afford a court battle with Dan, but she'd do anything within her power to keep Leah. There was no way she'd give him joint custody. At the very most, she'd allow him the right to come for a visit every now and then. She'd stick to her guns and not budge an inch.

She glanced at Leah who had rolled onto her back on the pink flowered quilt, her chubby legs kicking in the air, as she nibbled on her teething ring. "He doesn't deserve you," she whispered, holding back tears.

The only good news she had all week was that her mom was coming for a visit in a month. She's promised to help Brooke with her first paying guests and with any luck she'd be open for business by then. With Joe's expertise, her website would be operating soon and she'd managed to meet local merchants, hand out flyers and spread the word about her establishment.

"It's good news," she said to Leah. "I've gotta keep reminding myself that all this hard work will pay off one day."

Brooke got down on the floor and sat cross-legged on the quilt. She put Leah in a sitting position facing her. "Wanna play a game with Mommy?"

She took Leah's hands in hers and spread them wide. "Open," she said, drawing the word out. Then she closed their hands together, relaying in a sing-song voice, "Close them."

Leah giggled with joy. She loved this game. "Open," she repeated. "Close them." Brooke's mood lightened instantly just seeing her daughter's fascinated expression.

There was a sharp knock at the door, a knock she recognized. She braced herself, glancing outside at the parked car, before opening the door. Nick stood on the threshold, looking like a zillion bucks as usual and her heart thumped hard in her chest. He was eye-catching no matter what he wore, but today, he had on a tailored, and from the look of it, very expensive dark suit. "Hi," he said with a sparkling gleam in his blue eyes.

The sight of him blew her away. "Who died?"

He smiled. "You don't like my going-to-San-Francisco-on-business look?"

"You look nice, Nick," she relented, a gross understatement. "You didn't mention your trip this morning, though."

"It just came up. I'll be staying overnight. I came to give you the key to the house, just in case you miss Carlotta when you come in."

She let him in and they walked into the dining room. "Hey, kid," Nick said when he spotted Leah on the quilt. She gazed up at him and immediately lifted her arms for him to take her.

"She cut her first tooth. She's in a better mood today."

"Really," Nick said, taking off his jacket and getting down on the floor. "Let Nick see your tooth." He picked Leah up in his arms. Leah smiled at him, opening her mouth just slightly but not enough for him to catch a glimpse of it. He tickled her chin to make her laugh, then bent his head, searching until he came up with a grin. "Hey, there it is." He kissed Leah's forehead and Brooke's stomach twisted. How this man thought he wasn't good father material, she couldn't fathom. Granted, she'd thought so too, until she'd seen him interact with Leah and gotten to know him again.

Her heart broke thinking he'd never have a child of his own.

He looked up at Brooke, the smile still on his face. "Let's move furniture."

"What?"

"You have three more rooms to paint, don't you?"

"Yes, I was going to start on the next one when Leah took her nap this afternoon."

Nick rose, taking Leah in his arms. He tilted his chin and gestured upstairs. "It'll take me a few minutes."

"You're all dressed up."

"Are you going to stop arguing with me?" He glanced at Leah. "I hope you won't be this stubborn when you grow up."

Her daughter responded with a soft touch to his cheek.

"Okay, fine," she said. It was killing her seeing Nick holding Leah and how easy they were with each other. "Let's move furniture."

Half an hour later, after they'd arranged the furniture in the center of each of the three remaining rooms, Nick glanced at his watch. "I'd better get on the road. My meeting is in a couple of hours."

Brooke walked him downstairs and handed him his jacket. He slung it over his shoulder and strode to the door. "See you tomorrow night."

She nodded and glanced at his mouth.

He inhaled a sharp breath. "Keep looking at me that way and I'll never get out of here."

Heat rushed up her neck to warm her face. He was smooth, a charmer to the umpteenth degree, but he'd shown her a different side of himself last night and she feared she'd never get enough of him.

He took her into his arms and brushed a light kiss to her lips. Then he groaned and pulled her up tight against him, deepening the kiss. It lasted a gloriously long time and when they finally broke apart, both of them were breathing heavily.

"You make a man want to stay home nights," he whispered with a rasp, before turning and exiting the house.

She stood on the porch and watched him get into his car and pull out of the driveway. Then she entered the house and leaned back against the closed doorway. "Damn you, Nick. Don't say those things to me."

Nine

"So how long have you been teaching English at the high school?" Brooke asked Molly as they sat at the bed-and-breakfast's newly spruced up dining room table. It was tea for two with her aunt's Royal Albert English Chintz china teacups looking wonderful on the lacy rose tablecloth she'd laid out.

Molly juggled having Leah on her lap and sipping chamomile tea without the slightest pause. It was clear her friend knew a thing or two about children. She was glad she was finally able to have Molly over for an early brunch.

"This is my fifth year at the high school. I started teaching English and History a year after Adam was born and it's working out very well. We have our summers together and during the school season I'm home early. My husband works out of the house a few days a week, so he's Mr. Part-time Mom."

Brooke chuckled. "Is that what you call him?"

"Yeah, I do. John's got a great sense of humor. We laugh about it all the time."

"It's important to have someone to laugh with. Dan never laughed much. It's a wonder the two of us ever got together."

Molly reached for her hand. "You're doing the right thing by moving on. He wasn't right for you."

"Don't I know it! He'll be here in a couple of hours and I have no idea what I'm going to say to him."

"Just listen to what he says," Molly offered, touching her hand. "Let him speak his mind, but don't give him an answer. Tell him you have to think things over and then do that. There's no rush. You don't have to make any decisions quickly."

Having Molly here soothed her fragile nerves. She'd given her good advice and made her wish they hadn't lost touch with each other in the past. "Thanks, Molly. I will do that. It's the sane, rational thing to do." Then Brooke thought about it some more, shaking her head. "It's hard to be objective. He's such a snake."

A quick smile brought light to Molly's amber eyes. "Take the high road. Only call him a snake behind his back."

"I'll try," Brooke said, arching her brow as she pondered. "It won't be easy."

Brooke rose from her seat to arrange little round lemon pastries she'd made earlier this morning on a plate. She set out a bowl with fresh strawberries and raspberries topped with a special cream she'd prepared and a platter of sliced cranberry bread. "I'm practicing on you. Tell me what you think."

Molly tasted each one of the dishes and nodded. "Excellent. You get an A. The lemon tarts are amazing. When did you have time to do all this?"

"Last night and early this morning. Nick was gone, so I had free time."

Molly grinned. "Nick?"

"I mean, I usually cook him breakfast and dinner and the house was empty so I took advantage of the time to whip these up."

"Okay, I get it. He wasn't home to *occupy* your time, right?" Molly shot her a wicked smile. "What's up with the two of you?"

"He's a fr—" she began, then quickly stopped herself from calling him a friend. The "F" word wasn't a label she wanted between the two of them. "He and I have an arrangement. And no, it's not what you're thinking."

"Oh, so you're not sleeping with him? Too bad. Remember when he won Desert Island Dream in high school? The girls got to pick the one guy they'd like to be stranded on a desert island with."

"I remember," Brooke said with a groan. The girls wouldn't have been disappointed.

When Leah began to fidget too much, Molly set her down in her playpen and gave her a toy. "There you go."

Molly lifted up to stare into Brooke's eyes. "You had a thing for him and now you're living under his roof."

"Just temporarily. We'll be moving out soon. And he'll be off to Monte Carlo. He's got a house there and can't wait to leave the country."

Molly continued to stare at her, narrowing her eyes. "You're in love with him."

"I've got enough problems at the moment, thank you very much."

Molly spoke with gentle regard. "Doesn't change the fact."

"No, it doesn't," Brooke admitted, lowering her tea cup slowly to confess her innermost feelings. Maybe it would help to discuss this with someone. "It just happened. I had my eyes wide open, knowing it was impossible."

"To coin a cliché, love is blind. You can't help who you love."

"But you can be smart about it, can't you?"

Amusement sparked in Molly's eyes when she shook her head. "I don't think so. Intellect has very little to do with matters of the heart. Nick must be more than a hot hunk loaded with money for you to fall for him. The girl I knew needed more than eye candy." Molly was forever astute and that's why they'd gotten along in high school.

"Nick always let me see a side of him he rarely showed anyone else," Brooke said soberly. "I told myself over and over it was ridiculous and impossible, but there he was, opening up to me and being so good with Leah." Tears welled up in her eyes as she glanced at her baby sucking on her fist. Brooke had dressed her for company and she looked so pretty in her frilly flowered dress and bloomers. "Leah adores him."

She sniffed and halted her feelings of melancholy. "It's not going to work with him, Molly. My life is so complicated right now. I just want to have it all simple again."

Brooke and Molly talked for half an hour more and before her friend left she gave her a big comforting hug. "Call me anytime, Brooke."

"Don't worry, I will."

Brooke braced herself for Dan's visit. She didn't want this, any of it. She scooped Leah up in her arms and thought about running away, but it was just a wishful dream. She had to face him today and there wasn't much she could do about it. She sat down on the sofa and rocked Leah, giving her a bottle of formula and hoping she'd be sound asleep when Dan came by.

Less than an hour later, she heard a knock and rushed

to the door to keep Leah from waking up. "Come in," she said the second she saw Dan.

He entered the house. His hair was groomed, his face shaven, and he had on the same type of business casual clothes he always wore; khaki pants and a brown Polo shirt. She looked at him and felt nothing but disdain. At one time she had thought he was handsome, with his angular lines and sharp facial features. "Let's have a seat in the parlor."

She moved ahead of him and sat down in a wing chair that faced the sofa. Dan took the sofa and stared at her. He leaned forward. "You look good, Brooke. Pretty as always."

She refrained from rolling her eyes. "How did you know where we were?"

Dan glanced around the parlor taking it all in with assessing eyes as if doing mental calculations. "There's a lot of antiques in here. Are all the rooms furnished like this? How old is this place? "

"Old," she replied, refusing more information. "Please answer my question."

"Okay, fine, Brooke. I've been searching for you for months. I realized I'd made a drastic mistake. I hired a private detective to find you only to get a report last week that you'd had a baby and moved back to Napa."

"How touching," Brooke said. Was she supposed to cave just because he paid someone to find her?

Dan's face reddened and he looked ready to wrestle a bear.

She hoisted her chin.

"Look," he began. "Let's try to be civil to each other. We have a daughter."

Brooke hated hearing it. She hated that Leah had a drop of his blood and that he did have a legal right to see her. "Her name is Leah Marie and she's a Hamilton."

Dan's lips twisted. "She's a Hartley, Brooke, whether you want to accept it or not. Now, can I see her?"

Brooke's stomach quaked. "Fine, but please don't wake her." Brooke rose and took him into the downstairs bedroom where she'd set up a little crib she'd recently purchased on sale. Slowly, this place was becoming a home to them.

She led him into the bedroom and Dan gazed down at his daughter sleeping in the crib. He stood there a few minutes, just watching her as Brooke studied him. Something odd happened. Dan's expression didn't soften. It didn't change at all. His gaze didn't flow over Leah with loving adoration. Maybe it was because she was a stranger to him, or because he'd already lost one child, but Brooke had expected something more from Dan than the stony face staring down at the crib. Granted, he'd seen her several days ago, but that was for only a few seconds.

After half a minute, Brooke cleared her throat and Dan got the message. He exited the room with Brooke steps behind him.

"I remember you talking about this place," he said as they reentered the parlor and took their seats again. "Now it's all yours. What will you do with it?"

Brooke was taken aback by his question. Didn't he want to know about Leah? When was she born? How was the delivery? What is she like?

"I'm converting the house into a bed-and-breakfast. I have to support myself somehow."

"How many rooms does it have?"

"Eight, but six upstairs that I'll use for patrons."

"You were always good at homemaking, Brooke."

"Funny, but I never heard that from you before."

Dan gritted his teeth, making the words flowing from his mouth seem implausible. "I'm sorry I hurt you."

She wasn't sure that he really was. "That's not enough. Being sorry won't make up for anything. You abandoned me."

"I didn't know you were having a child. You should have told me."

"You shouldn't have gotten another woman pregnant and left me the way you did. You just packed up and moved out the same day I'd learned about it. I was in shock for months and picking up the pieces. I don't owe you anything, Dan."

"We can be a family again."

"That's not possible."

"Anything's possible, Brooke. Give us a second chance."

Leah cried out and Brooke prayed she'd fall back asleep, but the cries continued and she excused herself. "I have to get her. She's probably hungry and wet."

"I'll come with you."

"No. Stay here. I'll be back in a few minutes. I'll bring her in."

And Brooke walked out of the parlor on shaking legs.

Nick stepped onto Brooke's porch, a gift for Leah in one hand, another for Brooke in his pocket. He'd made it back to Napa after his late morning meeting with customers for Carlino Wines in good time and decided to stop by Brooke's house first before heading home this afternoon.

He told himself that Brooke might need a hand putting the furniture back in place after painting for the past two days, but in truth he was anxious to give the girls the gifts he'd picked up in San Francisco.

He heard a man speaking to Brooke from inside the house. The somber tone of his voice had an edge to it that

Nick didn't like. He pushed through the front door, without bothering to knock, and turned toward the parlor.

"Don't be unreasonable, Brooke," the man said. As he held Leah in his arms, the baby's lips turned down in a pout, tears ready to spill from her eyes. "Things could go so much easier if you agree to give us a second chance. I have rights and if you don't think so, I might have to take you to court."

Distressed, Brooke reached for her baby. "Give her to me, Dan. She's upset."

The man backed away from Brooke, refusing her the baby. "She needs to know her father."

"She *doesn't* know you and she's scared." Brooke said, panicked.

Nick stepped farther into the room, his emotions roiling. Seeing Leah in that man's arms and Brooke clearly agitated infuriated him. "Leah's not a pawn in this. Give her back the baby."

Both Brooke and Dan seemed startled to see him standing in the room.

"Who the hell are you?" Dan asked, raising his voice even more. He turned to Brooke, "Who is he and why is he issuing orders about my daughter?"

"Nick Carlino. He's been like a father to Leah, the only one she's ever known. She should be so lucky."

Nick's gaze darted straight to Brooke and from the firm resolve on her face he knew she meant what she said.

"But he's not her father. *I am.*"

The roughness of his voice carried across the room and Leah's face turned red as she burst into tears. The jerk was too selfish to realize he'd upset the baby.

"Give her to me," Brooke said quietly between gritted teeth.

"I will in a minute." Dan tried to calm Leah but it wasn't working, her cries grew louder.

Nick set Leah's gift down and strode up to Dan, his anger barely contained. Immediately, Leah turned toward him and reached out her wobbly arms, her sobs quieting down. Nick put his hands on Leah's waist, her body twisting toward him. He stared at Dan, his jaw tensing. "Let go of her."

The man glanced at Brooke then sighed. He released his hold on Leah. She flowed into Nick's arms. Her baby scent wafted up as she hung on tight, attaching herself to him. He held her for a few long moments and stroked her hair, before handing her back to Brooke. He eyed Leah's father with contempt and spoke with deadly calm. "Don't come in here and threaten them ever again."

"Nick, I can handle this," Brooke said, intervening. He didn't think so, but he backed off for her sake. "Dan was just leaving. We've said all we have to say for now."

"I'm not giving up, Brooke," Dan said. "We can make this work. I want you both back."

Brooke squeezed her eyes shut. "And I told you, that's not going to happen. Just go, Dan."

Dan shot a quick glance at Leah, then his gaze went to Brooke. "This isn't over." He sent Nick a hard look and strode out of the house with Nick at his heels. He waited until the guy was off the property before returning to Brooke, who had collapsed on the sofa with tears streaming down her face.

Nick stood staring at Brooke, his anger dissipating but other emotions clicking in with full force. When he'd walked into the house seeing another man holding Leah, claiming he wanted Brooke and Leah back in his life, surging waves of anger and jealousy destroyed his good mood. He'd never experienced anything like it, this fierce instinct to protect and comfort.

Brooke's defiant words from just minutes ago stuck in his head.

He's been like a father to Leah, the only one she's ever known.

Was that true? Was he getting that close to both Brooke and Leah? Or was Brooke just using those tactics with her ex to drive her point home, that Dan hadn't been any kind of father to Leah? He had walked out on Brooke and never looked back until what? What had happened to make him seek Brooke out?

She should be so lucky.

That comment had touched Nick in ways he didn't want to think about. Brooke couldn't possibly look at him as a role model for her child. Could she? Could she think of him in a way that he'd never thought of himself, as a man who could be a good father?

The *simple* they both wanted was getting real complicated.

His best bet would be to walk away now, but Nick knew he couldn't without helping Brooke one more time. He wouldn't leave until he was sure she and Leah would have the life they deserved. Dan had some rights to see his daughter, he was Leah's biological father, but Nick wouldn't stand by and watch the jerk hurt either of them.

He could be a hard-ass when necessary and this was the time and place for that.

Later that night, Nick watched as Brooke sat cross-legged on the floor opposite Leah in his living room, playing with the music box he'd brought home for the baby. Brooke opened the ornate silver box and a miniature ballerina twirled around to a classical tune that had Leah mesmerized. She kept trying to touch the ballerina and Brooke caught her hand each time. "Let the pretty ballerina dance," she said in a soft sweet voice.

Leah bobbed up and down with excitement from her sitting position and gurgled with laughter at the music box.

"She loves it, Nick."

Nick leaned forward in his chair, bracing elbows on knees, seeing Brooke finally calmed down from today's debacle. "Looks like it."

"Did you pick it out yourself?"

"I did. The ballerina reminded me of Leah."

Brooke's gaze met his. "You're an old softy."

"Just don't tell anyone."

Brooke glanced away for a few moments then turned to face him with regret. "I'm sorry you had to witness that today."

"I'm not. I seriously hope you don't plan on letting that guy back into your life."

"Not if I can help it," Brooke said, closing the music box. "But what choice do I have if he takes me to court?"

"He won't do that." Nick had connections and already had someone on it. He'd managed to memorize Dan Hartley's license plate and coupled with the information he'd gathered from conversations with Brooke, he'd know a lot more about him and his motives very soon. "How much are you willing to give him as far as Leah goes?"

"Nothing, but I have to be realistic. She may want to know her father one day. At the very most, I'd grant him visitation rights with me being there. That's all I can imagine for now."

"That might be doable."

"I'm not that sure, Nick. I'm going to have a lot of sleepless nights over this."

"He's the reason you came to me that first night, isn't it?" It didn't take a rocket scientist to figure that one out. "You were upset."

"That was part of the reason," she confessed with apology in her voice.

Nick arched his brows. "Part? What was the other part?"

"Maybe you're just irresistible."

Nick scoffed at that. "Come on, Brooke. Tell me."

Indecision marred her pretty face as she debated a few seconds before finally owning up. "It was partly because Dan had contacted me and I was frightened, but it was also because I wanted to be reckless for once in my life. I wanted something just for me. I've dreamed about being with you for a long time and well, you were just down the hall giving me an open invitation."

Nick swallowed down hard. He didn't know what to say to that.

"I know you're leaving, and I've got my own plans. I figured no harm could come of it."

"You want simple, I get that," he said. "I've lived my whole life that way."

"Right. Simple is as simple does."

Only Brooke and Leah were complicating the hell out of his life lately.

Nick stood and walked over to Brooke, reaching for her hand and when she placed it in his, he helped her up. He wound his arms around her waist and kissed her gently. "It's late. You've had a rough day. Let's go to bed."

"Together?" she asked.

"I'll be waiting for you."

Brooke's eyes softened and she smiled. "As soon as I get the baby to sleep, I'll be there."

Nick would hold her all night long if that was what

she wanted. He'd never done that with a woman but with Brooke, all his rules were shot to hell.

He picked up Leah and walked up the stairs side by side with Brooke, Nick kissing the baby's cheek before handing her off to her mommy.

He was in deep. But he hadn't changed his mind about anything. Brooke knew the score—he was leaving for Monte Carlo in just a few weeks.

He wanted no ties to Napa at all and that included this beautiful blond mommy with her equally beautiful blond baby.

Brooke got Leah to sleep easily. All that crying today had worn her out. She checked on her one last time, before she donned the oversized T-shirt that Nick liked and went to his room. She knocked softly and Nick was there, immediately opening the door and taking her into his arms. He held her gently and kissed her forehead, cheek and chin before bringing his warm inviting lips to hers.

"I don't think I can leave Leah," she whispered, a sense of urgency she couldn't explain, niggling at her. "I'm sorry. I thought I could, but I can't. It's going to be hard enough for me to fall asleep tonight."

Nick kissed her forehead again. "Then I'll come to you."

She gazed into his eyes.

He winked and pulled her against his chest. "I miss my big old bed."

"I'm not feeling—"

"I know, honey. We'll just *sleep* together. Just don't tell anybody, it might ruin my reputation."

She punched him in the shoulder. "You're so bad, Nick." Then she added, "In a wonderful way."

A chuckle rumbled from his chest. "That might be the nicest thing you've ever said to me."

She turned to go back to her bedroom, but Nick grabbed her hand just in time and she swirled around to face him. "Wait a second." He moved to the dresser and pulled out a black velvet box from the top drawer. "When I saw this, I knew you had to have it."

He handed her the square box. "This is for you."

Her heart pounded and she was totally confused. "What, why?"

"Open it, Brooke."

She held the box with trembling hands and opened it slowly. "Oh, Nick, this is beautiful." She fingered the green-blue oval gemstone surrounded by inset diamonds on a long silver chain.

"It's tourmaline. This stone is the exact color of your eyes."

"I don't know what to say, except thank you...and why?"

Nick shrugged. "Why not? When I saw the necklace it reminded me of you and I wanted you to have it."

"But it's probably worth more than my old clunker car."

"Your point?"

"I don't really have one, except that it's too generous, Nick. You've already done so much for me. How can I possibly accept this?"

He gave her a smoldering kiss, loving her mouth and charming her into submission. "Just say you love it."

She shook her head, ready to refuse his gift even after that mind-blowing kiss. She had pride and Nick had given her so much already, but she couldn't insult him by not accepting such a thoughtful gesture. Happy tears pooled in her eyes. "You're impossible, you know."

"I've heard that before."

She reached up on tiptoes and pressed a sweet kiss to his lips. "I love it. But you shouldn't have done it."

"I do a lot of things I shouldn't do, but giving you this gift isn't one of them."

Nick put out the light and took her hand, leading her back to the master bedroom. Quietly, they slipped in between the sheets and he took her into his arms and held her until she fell asleep.

Brooke woke early in the morning in a better mood. She'd had a good night's rest after all, cradled next to Nick during the night. She breathed in his expensive musky cologne and smiled from ear to ear at the position they were in. He lay on his back, his legs spread out, while she was on her stomach, her thigh thrust over his, and his full thick erection pressing against her hip.

"It's about time you woke up," he said, stroking her back.

Stunned, she let out a gasp. "How long have you been like this?"

Nick groaned a complaint. "Too long. Am I taking a cold shower this morning?"

Brooke kissed his neck and whispered, "Sometimes that can be fun when we do it together."

"Brooke," he warned then he rolled her over onto her back and kissed her until her lips burned from the scorching heat. He gazed into her eyes until she nodded and smiled. He wasn't a man to be denied, not that Brooke could even conceive of that now. She wanted him in all the ways that complicated her life. She wanted him in any way she could have him.

Nick made love to her with slow hands and sexy words that sent her mind spinning and her body aching for more. He was an expert at making a woman feel desirable and beautiful. She relished every illicit touch, every gliding stroke of his hands and every moist sensual thrust of his tongue.

With his encouragement she touched him back, her assault a partial revenge for the tortured pleasure he'd given her. She inched her palms up his muscled chest, through the coarse hairs surrounding his nipples. She kissed him there, then suckled on him until a heavy impatient groan erupted in his throat. She smiled and moved farther up, kissing him hard then outlining his mouth with her index finger, swirling it around and around, then slipping it into his mouth. He suckled her finger and pressure built, his chest heaving as much as hers. Heavy heat consumed her and when Nick held her tight and rolled her on top of him, instincts took over.

He helped her off with her T-shirt and she slid him out of his boxers. Naked now and consumed with lust, Brooke took his thick shaft in her hands and stroked him, sliding her open palm up and down the silken skin. She bent and put her mouth on him, loving him with fiery passion. She sensed when he was at the brink and rose above him. His face was emblazoned with desire, his rough stubble and dark hair tousled. He was the sexiest man alive.

She lowered her body down in a straddle and took him inside her. It felt so right, so perfect that she wanted to cry. Nick watched her ride him, his eyes heavy-lidded. He brought his hands to her breasts and caressed her, sensitizing her pebble-hard nipples even more. She ached for him, wanted him and loved him like no other man before.

Her climax came first and she splintered, her nerves tight, her body convulsing and finally giving up to the intense pleasure of being joined with Nick.

Nick watched her with awe in his eyes and when she was completely through, she rolled off him and accommodated his weight. He filled her again and she welcomed him. He thrust into her hard and fast, his climax coming just seconds after hers. She felt another wave of fulfillment just witnessing the satisfaction she could give to him.

She was so much in love with him her heart ached.

Afterward, they lay in each other's arms silently.

Brooke felt content and happy, but distraught at the same time. She knew this wouldn't last. She knew she was in for a gigantic fall.

When Leah made her early rising sounds, little complaints as she woke, Brooke lifted up to get her. Nick put a stopping hand on her arm. "I'll get her."

Brooke shook her head. "She'll need to be changed."

Nick winced, his lips pulling down in a frown. "Really?"

"Of course, really. She's slept all night in the same diaper."

Nick thought about it for half a second then gave her a quick kiss on the lips, slipped on his boxers and rose from the bed. "I'll take care of it. Just relax."

Brooke laid her head down on the pillow and grinned as she heard Nick struggling with the diaper change, but after a while Nick brought Leah to her. "Here she is."

He sat Leah on the bed between the two of them and Brooke inspected his handiwork. "Well, you're no speed demon, but it looks good."

With a satisfied look on his face, he winked. "I learned from the best."

She hated when Nick said nice things. She hated when he did nice things. And he'd been doing and saying nice things for so long now. Maybe she should have clung to her anger and not let him charm her into liking him. Because aside from being head-over-heels in love, she really liked the man Nick had become.

Deep down in her heart, Brooke knew this wasn't a good idea. Nick hadn't made her any promises. He'd been up front and honest with her. She was the one who wanted "simple."

What she'd gotten was a whole lot more.

Sure, she feared Leah was getting too attached to Nick. But her mommy was already a terribly hopeless case.

Ten

Three days later, Nick showed up unannounced at the bed-and-breakfast just as Brooke had finished dusting the entire house from top to bottom. She met him at the front door, wearing an apron with her hair pulled back in a ponytail. "Hi," she said, looking at him with confusion. "You didn't say you were stopping by this morning."

"I have some news," he said, his face grim. He made his way into the house and walked into the kitchen. Brooke followed him inside the room, curious. He gestured to a chair. "Here, have a seat."

Brooke's heart pounded with dread as he waited for her to sit down. "What is it?"

He sat in a chair adjacent to her. "I had your ex investigated. Don't ask me how or why, but it's done."

Brooke ran a hand down her face, taking it all in. She was more than a little stunned. "Okay," she dragged out, "but I don't understand."

"He's bankrupt. Seems his girlfriend cleaned him out and he's desperate for money. He knew that you'd had his child, months before showing up here."

Brooke blinked and shook her head. "What are you saying?"

Nick studied her face and spoke quietly, "I'm saying that he didn't search for you for months. He found out where you were right after Leah was born. He knew about her almost from the time of her birth. He didn't come for you and Leah, until he found out that you inherited this house. The house is probably worth what, three quarters of a million dollars? He probably figured you'd inherited a huge pile of cash along with it."

Brooke squeezed her eyes shut momentarily. "That bastard."

When she opened her eyes again, she saw the whole startling truth. It hurt to know what little she'd ever meant to Dan, but it hurt worse knowing he didn't really care about his daughter. "He was after my money?" Brooke asked, already certain of the answer.

Nick nodded.

Her heart in her throat and her stomach in knots, she was ready to cry. "It's hard to believe I once loved him. Shows you what a poor judge of character I am."

"Don't beat yourself up too badly. He only showed you a side of himself he wanted you to see."

"He's Leah's father and she deserves more."

"He won't be around much."

Brooke snapped her head up and stared into eyes that didn't meet hers. "What did you do? You didn't make him disappear, did you?"

Nick cast her a crooked grin and scratched the back of his neck. "No, I had a little chat with him. I told him you and Leah were off-limits. You'll decide when and where you want Leah to see him."

"How did you get him to agree…?" Then it dawned on Brooke. "Oh Nick, you paid him off, didn't you?"

Nick kept his expression unreadable. "All that matters is that you and Leah won't be bothered by him from now on."

"It does matter." Brooke rose from her chair. "How much was my little girl worth to him? How could he put a price tag on that?"

Nick stood and cupped her shoulders in his big hands, holding her still while she wanted to throw things. He spoke calmly. "It doesn't matter, Brooke. He was never in Leah's life. You can move on and forget about him. Will you do that?"

Brooke stared at Nick, wondering if she should take that same advice about him. She was a bad judge of character. She'd fallen for a guy who'd flat out told her he didn't want a family—a man who was leaving to live halfway across the world. Was he also telling her to move on and forget about him?

Nick's cell phone rang and he excused himself to answer it. Brooke took that time to check on Leah, then wash her face and comb her hair. She removed her apron and by the time Nick reentered the kitchen, she had new but heartbreaking determination.

"That was Tony. He's a giddy mess. Rena had the baby. They named him David Anthony Carlino." Nick's grin broadened across his face.

Brooke's heavy heart warmed. Babies brought such joy into a person's life. "That's wonderful. Is Rena okay?"

"According to my big brother, she's doing fine. I'm going to see them now. Want to come?"

"No, no. You go. Tell Rena I'll visit her another time. I want to see the baby. But this time is for family."

The thought of seeing Rena, Tony and their new baby, a child that wasn't Tony's biological child but one he'd love like his own, hit a little too close to home. Brooke had wanted that so much for herself, but it wasn't to be. And after the news she'd gotten today about Dan, she couldn't take witnessing the happy threesome with their whole future ahead of them.

Nick cast her an odd look. "She wouldn't mind if you came with me."

"No, Nick," she said with resolve. "I'm not coming with you. I'm not part of your family."

And I never will be.

That night when Brooke entered the Carlino house, her courage bolstered by the words she'd rehearsed all day and knew by heart, she found Nick's suitcase by the front door.

"Hi," Nick said, coming to greet her when she walked in. "You should have seen the size of that baby. He was almost nine pounds." He held two flutes of champagne. "I've been waiting for you to celebrate."

Leah clung to her shoulder, nearly asleep. "I can't right now, Nick. Leah's not feeling well. She's a little warm and her nose is running. I'm going to put her to sleep."

Nick's face fell and she could barely stand to watch his cheerful expression transform. He gazed at Leah with concern, his eyes soft and caring. "I'll go up with you." He set the flutes down, ready to help.

"No, that's okay. She's a little clingy right now. Are you going somewhere?"

Nick glanced at the suitcase in the entry. "I've got a

crisis at the Monte Carlo house. I'm leaving on the red-eye tonight. I hope to be back in three days, tops."

Brooke stopped when she reached the base of the staircase and seized on her chance to say her rehearsed words. "Nick, now's as good a time as any to tell you, Leah and I are moving out. The house is ready for us now. I don't have much more to do before I can open my doors. We'll be gone before you get back."

Nick furrowed his brows. "You're leaving?" He sounded as if it were news to him. This had always been their deal, though it broke her heart to see the look of confusion on his face. Women didn't walk out on Nick Carlino.

"It's time for me to go. I want to thank you for everything. I don't know what I would've done without your help these past few weeks. I promise, I'll find a way to pay you back. And I'm still in shock about how you handled Dan. I don't know what to say about that."

"Damn it, Brooke, you don't owe me anything." His mouth tightened to a thin line. "And you don't have to move out right now."

"Yes, Nick. I do. That was the deal." He was the classic dealmaker in the family, so he should understand. She may owe him a few weeks of work, but he'd just have to make do. She couldn't live in the house with him another day. "This was always a temporary arrangement."

His eyes darkened with anger. "I know that."

"I've learned something since coming back to Napa, Nick. You can't dwell on the past. You have to move on and look to the future. You've helped me see that."

Nick stared at her without blinking.

"Just think, you'll have the house back to normal, no more baby things to trip over."

Nick ignored her little jest. "This is because of what that jerk did to you, isn't it?"

Brooke smiled with sadness in her heart and shook her head. How could she explain that her leaving had nothing to do with Dan and everything to do with protecting herself and her daughter from getting attached to Nick, a man who was bent on running away from his past, a man who wanted a lifestyle that didn't include a ready-made family. "You've given me so much and I want to return the favor the only way I know how. My friend Molly says the high school is in desperate need of a baseball coach for the boys. You should think about it."

Nick looked at her like she'd gone crazy.

"Okay," she said with a heavy sigh. Saying good-bye to Nick was one of the hardest things she'd ever had to do. She summoned all her courage and held her ground, when she wanted to throw herself into his arms. "I've got to go up. Leah and I have a long day tomorrow." She whispered softly, "Good-bye, Nick."

Nick remained silent. She sensed his gaze on her as she climbed the stairs to the room she'd sleep in one last time. When she reached the top of the staircase, she heard him pick up his suitcase and open the front door.

There was a long pause before finally, the front door slammed shut.

Silent tears rained down her face as she carried her precious child to her bed. Brooke had no one to blame but herself. She'd come into this with her eyes wide open yet couldn't help falling in love with him again regardless of her constant internal warnings.

But by far, this time hurt the most.

She'd never get over Nick Carlino.

Not in this lifetime.

Nick sat on the deck of his Monte Carlo home and sipped wine, gazing out at the Mediterranean's classic blue waters.

He had everything he wanted here, a gorgeous view of the ocean, twelve rooms of modern conveniences and old world charm, friends to party with and a world-renowned casino only minutes away.

He'd gambled there last night and had gone out with friends afterward. He had offers from women during his time here, but Nick wasn't interested in them. Somehow their sleek clothes and sultry looks didn't stir his juices as they once had. Images of Brooke in her mommy clothes would seep into his mind instead. But he balked at that.

Thoughts of her stayed with him constantly, but he knew that would pass. Nick wanted an easy life and now that he was away from all that Napa represented, he decided to stay on a few more days.

The Italian marble "crisis" his contractor had called him about had been straightened out and it turned out not to be a big deal after all. The renovations he'd ordered were almost done and not a minute too soon. He was only weeks from winning his bet with his brothers, and by all accounts he'd already won. He'd be through with his father's wine business once and for all and he could come and go as he pleased. He would enjoy rubbing his brothers' faces in the win, smug as they both had been about the bet.

But with those thoughts also came Brooke's words that she'd spoken just days ago. *You can't dwell on the past. You have to move on and look to the future.*

He'd helped her see that?

A smile spread across his face. If he had, then he was damn glad. He couldn't deny that he wanted to see her happy. She'd always been special to him and she always made him smile with her sassy tongue and witty comebacks. She had a chance for a good future with Leah now.

During the next few days, Nick refused more party invitations than he accepted and he refrained from entertaining females at the house. He took walks on the beach, spent a more active role in the renovations and watched sports on television.

After dinner on Thursday night, he placed a call to Rena and Tony. The baby was almost a week old and Uncle Nick wanted to hear how the three of them were doing.

Rena picked up and said hello.

"Hi, it's Nick. I'm checking on my favorite uncle status."

"You're still it, but don't tell Joe I said so. And least *he* isn't thousands of miles away. He didn't abandon the family."

Nick chuckled at Rena's teasing.

"I'll be back in few days and I'm bringing gifts."

"Oh, so you're spoiling my child already?"

"That's the plan. How's the little guy?"

"He's doing fine. Eating like a Carlino and growing like one too. I never knew breast-feeding could be so challenging."

Nick laughed and an image popped into his head of Brooke holding Leah to her breast, the baby nursing until she was good and satisfied. The serene picture they'd made would be forever imbedded in his mind. "I bet you could ask Brooke for advice. She seemed to take to it naturally."

"Brooke?" Rena paused. "That girl's got her hands full right now."

"What do you mean?"

"You haven't heard?"

"No, I haven't spoken with her. We don't have that kind of relationship," Nick said, convincing himself of that fact.

"The baby's in the hospital."

"What?" Nick's good mood vanished. His heart pounded hard and he thought he heard wrong. "Leah's in the hospital?"

"Yes, she had a febrile seizure."

"A seizure?" Nick couldn't believe it. "But she's such a healthy kid."

"It's caused from a high temperature. The baby was sick and her fever spiked really fast. It's pretty scary, but they say it happens to some children. Because she's so young, they're doing tests to make sure it's nothing more serious."

"Damn! It better not be." Nick couldn't fathom that sweet baby having to suffer. "How's Brooke?"

"She's a brave one. She's all alone and I tell you, I don't know how she does it. Ali stopped by the hospital when she found out to check on both of them. She said Brooke is holding up. She has no choice, but it's rough. Her world revolves around that baby."

"Oh man." Nick put his head down and took a few deep breaths. His stomach felt hollowed out, like someone had gone in and scooped out his guts with a shovel.

"You should call her, Nick. She doesn't say it, but I know she misses you."

"I'm not so sure." He couldn't call her. He didn't know what to say to her. He'd walked out on her just like every other man in her life. He'd let her down and he'd done it without realizing it. He should have known better than to get involved with someone like Brooke. She didn't need him in her life. She needed stability. She needed someone who would be there for her, through thick and thin. She needed a man who would love the hell out of her and her beautiful daughter.

He's been like a father to Leah. She should be that lucky.

Had Brooke meant it? Had she seen something in him that he hadn't seen in himself?

Nick hung up the phone and paced the length of his living room, darting glances around his home, noting the textured walls and marble flooring, the pillared terrace with its sweeping vista overlooking the Mediterranean. The place was perfect. He'd gotten what he wanted. He could Pass Go and Collect $200 and as an added bonus he'd received the Get Out of Jail Free card, his prison being Napa and all it signified.

He admitted that he had decided to stay on longer in Monte Carlo to keep as much distance from Brooke as possible. She would have moved out of his house by now. He could go back to living his bachelor life, yet he didn't like what he was feeling about her. He missed her, but he was no good for her. He wouldn't succumb to those emotions. A few more days away would help purge her from his thoughts.

"Hang on, Nick," he muttered to himself. "Don't go nuts because the kid got sick. Brooke's a survivor. She'll be okay."

And to prove to himself that he was better off without them and vice-versa, he went out that night. He gambled in Monaco and had dinner with an acquaintance he'd met months ago at the roulette table. She was beautiful and willing, but he made up an excuse and spent the night alone in his bed.

Nick woke up feeling like crap. If someone had taken a hammer to his head, he couldn't feel worse. The hell of it was, he knew why. He hadn't caught too many winks last night and he had two blond-haired, blue-eyed females to thank for that. He rose from his bed and padded to the kitchen for some aspirin.

Only Nick knew beyond a doubt now, aspirin wouldn't cure what was really wrong with him.

Brooke took Leah out of her car seat in the back of the Lexus and gazed at her daughter with pride. "You're my pretty girl." Leah returned her compliment with a two-toothed smile. She'd dressed her in a brand-new white dress dotted with bright red cherries and green stems. Atop her baby blond curls sat a cherry red bow.

"We're going to visit your new little friend, David Anthony today," she said as she walked up the path to the house at Purple Fields. Brooke had dressed to match Leah. She wore a red and white sundress, minus the cherries. It felt good to dress up for a change and go out with Leah. Since the move into the bed-and-breakfast, Brooke had felt somewhat isolated and lonely, just the two of them in that big house.

Leah's medical episode had taken its toll on Brooke. The febrile seizure had come on so suddenly and had scared her half to death. She'd called the paramedics and they'd taken Leah to the hospital. By the time they arrived, Leah was alert and awake again. The doctor explained that the seizure was the body's natural reaction to such high temperatures and as soon as Leah's body adjusted, she came out of it. They also explained that febrile seizures in themselves were not life threatening.

Thank God for that.

They'd kept Leah in the hospital to do some tests and when they released her with a clean bill of health, Brooke had broken down and cried her eyes out. Now, just three days later, Leah was a happy girl again and both were looking forward to spending time with Rena and the new baby.

She knocked on the door and just a few seconds later Rena appeared, looking beautiful and well rested. "Hi, Rena. Leah and I are so excited to see you and the baby."

"I'm glad you accepted the invitation." Rena smiled at her and patted Leah's head. "She looks happy and healthy, Brooke. Is all okay now?"

"Yes, she's perfect. Thanks for your support and friendship. It means a lot to me."

Rena opened the door wider. "Come in, please."

Brooke stepped into the entrance hall and followed Rena to the living room. Once they reached it, Rena turned to her with apology in her eyes. "I just want you to know this wasn't my idea. I think there's a better way to do this."

Puzzled, Brooke looked at Rena then followed the line of her gaze into the room. Tony, Joe and Ali were there. "Oh, I didn't realize you were having the family over."

Rena sighed and shot Tony a hard look.

"Meet little David Anthony." Tony walked over to greet them and Brooke forgot all else, thrilled to see their new child.

"He's beautiful. You must be so happy."

"We are," Tony said to her, then Rena walked over and Tony put his arm around her. "We're thrilled."

Leah reached a hand out to touch the baby and Brooke made sure she was gentle, helping guide her hand to his cheek. "Isn't he sweet, Leah?" And after they'd fawned over little David, Brooke turned to say hello to Ali and Joe. They inquired about Leah's health and made her feel welcome, then the room became awkwardly silent. Brooke wondered what was up.

"Sorry, Brooke," Ali said finally.

Rena joined forces with Ali. "We didn't know about the bet."

Brooke looked from one woman to the other, sensing their discomfort and feeling some of her own. "What bet? What's going on?"

Nick appeared, coming out of another room and startling her. He stood in a solid stance, his gaze flowing over her from head to toe with hunger in his eyes, then he glanced at Leah and his gaze went heartbreakingly soft. He looked drop-dead gorgeous and dangerously confident about something. Just seeing him again squeezed her heart and coiled her stomach. He'd hurt her when he hadn't called about Leah. He must have known. He must have realized how much agony she'd been in when Leah was sick. He'd taken her at her word when she'd asked for *simple,* but she never thought he'd be so cold and uncaring. He should have called and asked about Leah.

"Hello, Brooke," he said.

She couldn't keep her disappointment from showing. She pursed her lips.

"Tell her," Nick demanded, looking at his brothers.

Joe glanced at Nick. "You're sure? This could spell doom for you, bro."

Nick nodded. "I want her to know the truth, all of it."

Tony handed the baby off to Rena and she shook her head at him. "We were on your side, Brooke. In all of this," Tony said in a defensive tone.

"All of what? What's going on?" she asked.

As soon as Leah spotted Nick, she put her arms out to him and she bounced with excitement until Brooke could barely contain her. "Leah!"

The dimples of doom broke out on Nick's face and he strode over to Brooke. "Let me hold her."

"I can't seem to stop her," she said, disgruntled.

Leah reached out for Nick and when he took her, she clung to his neck. He kissed her cheek and stroked her hair. "Thank God you're all right."

Ali's and Rena's expressions softened.

"Tell her the truth," Nick demanded again of his brothers.

"Why don't you tell me, Nick?" Brooke said, angrily. "Since it's obvious this was all set up and your doing. Tell me what you have to say."

Nick looked at his brothers who refused to speak. "Cowards."

"On that note, we'll leave you two alone." Joe grabbed Ali's hand and walked outside.

"That's a good plan. Let's take the baby for a walk," Tony said to Rena and the three of them left the room.

Once they were alone, Nick turned to her. "Okay, I'll tell you the truth. When you first came to live with me after your accident, my brothers were so damn sure I'd get involved with you. I mean, here you were vulnerable and alone and you had this adorable kid. They were so damn smug about it. I told them what I told you, I don't do permanent and I'm not father material. I was so sure of how I felt," he said, stroking her daughter's hair again, "that I made them a wager. I bet them I wouldn't fall for you and want the whole enchilada. I bet them my stake in the company. If I didn't fall in love with you, I get a free pass with Carlino Wines. I wouldn't have to run the company and I wouldn't have to stay in Napa. I'd be out of the running and it would be between Joe and Tony."

Brooke's mouth dropped open and she was stunned speechless.

Nick went on, "I told you how much I hated it here. How much I wanted revenge against my father. So much so, that I wanted nothing to do with his legacy. So much so, that I couldn't see past my anger. But you made me see things differently, Brooke. You made me realize that I shouldn't live in the past. That's all I've been doing, living in the past and running away."

Brooke regained her composure and finally spoke. "You actually *bet* you wouldn't fall in love with me? Not very good for a girl's ego, is it?"

"I wasn't looking for permanent, Brooke. But man, was I wrong. I lost the bet. I'm the new head of Carlino

Wines. I'm the CEO now and rightfully so. Joe and Tony are staying on too. We're brothers and we're going to help each other. Thanks to you I'm facing my past and moving on to my future."

Brooke swallowed hard. "Nick." She didn't know what to say.

"I put in a call to the high school too. Looks like they might want me to coach the Victors this season."

"Oh, Nick. That's wonderful."

"You've made it all possible, Brooke. You helped me see that I was wasting my life away. This is one bet I was glad to lose. Because I'm crazy about you and Leah. You're all that matters to me. I don't want to lose you and if it means me staying in Napa and running the company, I'll do it. I want you that much. I love you that much."

Brooke got past the initial ego deflation, to hear him, to really hear what he was telling her. He loved her. He loved Leah. It was quite a lot to take in. He was making sacrifices for her and the idea warmed her to the point of melting. "What's the whole enchilada?"

Nick spoke with reverence and a hopeful tone. "Marriage. The three of us being a family, everything I thought I never wanted."

"And now you do?"

"I took the CEO position to prove it to you." He lowered his voice and spoke with sincerity. "With your help, I think I could be a good father to Leah."

Oh my God. That did it. Any anger she felt over the stupid bet he made just faded to nothingness. She couldn't hold it against him. He'd always been honest with her. But hearing him say he loved her and that he wanted to be Leah's father turned her insides to jelly. Tears welled in her eyes and raw emotion overwhelmed her. She struggled to get the words out yet she felt them with every beat of her heart, "You don't need my help being a good father. Leah's already crazy about you."

"What about you, Brooke? How do you feel about me? Still trying to keep it simple?"

Her smile spread across her face and her heart burst with joy. "Nick, you've complicated my life since the day I set eyes on you in high school. I loved you then and I love you now."

Nick breathed in deep. "Then will you marry me?"

Brooke gazed at him holding Leah in his arms. "You don't play fair asking me with Leah looking at you like you could paint the moon."

"I could, with both of you in my life."

Brooke sighed with utter joy and spoke the words she'd never thought she'd ever say to Nick Carlino. "Yes, I'll marry you."

Nick bundled her up close, the three of them in a huddle and Nick kissed her with sweet tenderness. "I've missed you, Brooke. I've missed you both. I promised you that night of the crash that I'd take care of Leah. I want to do that and share my life with you. We'll be a family, the three of us."

"Oh, Nick. That's all I've ever wanted."

Brooke would have the family she'd always hoped for, but she was getting a bonus.

Her very own drop-dead handsome, dangerously sexy Desert Island Dream.

What more could a girl ask for?

* * * * *

COMING NEXT MONTH

Available October 12, 2010

#2041 ULTIMATUM: MARRIAGE
Ann Major
Man of the Month

#2042 TAMING HER BILLIONAIRE BOSS
Maxine Sullivan
Dynasties: The Jarrods

#2043 CINDERELLA & THE CEO
Maureen Child
Kings of California

#2044 FOR THE SAKE OF THE SECRET CHILD
Yvonne Lindsay
Wed at Any Price

#2045 SAVED BY THE SHEIKH!
Tessa Radley

#2046 FROM BOARDROOM TO WEDDING BED?
Jules Bennett

REQUEST YOUR FREE BOOKS!

2 FREE NOVELS PLUS 2 FREE GIFTS!

Silhouette® Desire®

Passionate, Powerful, Provocative!

YES! Please send me 2 FREE Silhouette Desire® novels and my 2 FREE gifts (gifts are worth about $10). After receiving them, if I don't wish to receive any more books, I can return the shipping statement marked "cancel." If I don't cancel, I will receive 6 brand-new novels every month and be billed just $4.05 per book in the U.S. or $4.74 per book in Canada. That's a saving of at least 15% off the cover price! It's quite a bargain! Shipping and handling is just 50¢ per book.* I understand that accepting the 2 free books and gifts places me under no obligation to buy anything. I can always return a shipment and cancel at any time. Even if I never buy another book, the two free books and gifts are mine to keep forever.

225/326 SDN E5QG

Name _____ (PLEASE PRINT)

Address _____ Apt. #

City _____ State/Prov. _____ Zip/Postal Code

Signature (if under 18, a parent or guardian must sign) _____

Mail to the **Silhouette Reader Service:**
IN U.S.A.: P.O. Box 1867, Buffalo, NY 14240-1867
IN CANADA: P.O. Box 609, Fort Erie, Ontario L2A 5X3

Not valid for current subscribers to Silhouette Desire books.

Want to try two free books from another line?
Call 1-800-873-8635 or visit www.morefreebooks.com.

* Terms and prices subject to change without notice. Prices do not include applicable taxes. N.Y. residents add applicable sales tax. Canadian residents will be charged applicable provincial taxes and GST. Offer not valid in Quebec. This offer is limited to one order per household. All orders subject to approval. Credit or debit balances in a customer's account(s) may be offset by any other outstanding balance owed by or to the customer. Please allow 4 to 6 weeks for delivery. Offer available while quantities last.

Your Privacy: Silhouette Books is committed to protecting your privacy. Our Privacy Policy is available online at www.eHarlequin.com or upon request from the Reader Service. From time to time we make our lists of customers available to reputable third parties who may have a product or service of interest to you. If you would prefer we not share your name and address, please check here. ☐

Help us get it right—We strive for accurate, respectful and relevant communications. To clarify or modify your communication preferences, visit us at www.ReaderService.com/consumerchoice.

SDES10R

HARLEQUIN®

A Romance

FOR EVERY MOOD™

Spotlight on

Heart & Home

Heartwarming romances
where love can happen
right when you least expect it.

See the next page to enjoy a sneak peek
from Harlequin Superromance®,
a Heart and Home series.

CATHHHSR10

Enjoy a sneak peek at fan favorite Molly O'Keefe's
Harlequin Superromance miniseries,
THE NOTORIOUS O'NEILLS, *with*
TYLER O'NEILL'S REDEMPTION,
available September 2010
only from Harlequin Superromance.

Police chief Juliette Tremblant recognized the shape of the man strolling down the street—in as calm and leisurely fashion as if it were the middle of the day rather than midnight. She slowed her car, convinced her eyes were playing tricks on her. It had been a long time since Tyler O'Neill had been seen in this town.

As she pulled to a stop at the curb, he turned toward her, and her heart about stopped.

"What the hell are you doing here, Tyler?"

"Well, if it isn't Juliette Tremblant." He made his way over to her, then leaned down so he could look her in the eye. He was close enough to touch.

Juliette was not, repeat, *not* going to touch Tyler O'Neill. Not with her fingers. Not with a ten-foot pole. There would be no touching. Which was too bad, since it was the only way she was ever going to convince herself the man standing in front of her—as rumpled and heart-stoppingly handsome now as he'd been at sixteen—was real.

And not a figment of all her furious revenge dreams.

"What are you doing back in Bonne Terre?" she asked.

"The manor is sitting empty," Tyler said and shrugged, as though his arriving out of the blue after ten years was casual. "Seems like someone should be watching over the family home."

"You?" She laughed at the very notion of him being here for any unselfish reason. "Please."

He stared at her for a second, then smiled. Her heart fluttered against her chest—a small mechanical bird powered by that smile.

"You're right." But that cryptic comment was all he offered.

Juliette bit her lip against the other questions.

Why did you go?

Why didn't you write? Call?

What did I do?

But what would be the point? Ten years of silence were all the answer she really needed.

She had sworn off feeling anything for this man long ago. Yet one look at him and all the old hurt and rage resurfaced as though they'd been waiting for the chance. That made her mad.

She put the car in gear, determined not to waste another minute thinking about Tyler O'Neill. "Have a good night, Tyler," she said, liking all the cool "go screw yourself" she managed to fit into those words.

It seems Juliette has an old score to settle with Tyler.
Pick up TYLER O'NEILL'S REDEMPTION
to see how he makes it up to her.
Available September 2010,
only from Harlequin Superromance.

Copyright © 2010 by Molly Fader

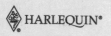

INTRIGUE

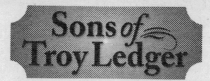

Five brothers, one mystery

JOANNA WAYNE

brings an all-new suspenseful series of five
brothers searching for the truth behind their
mother's murder and their father's unknown past.

Will their journey allow them
to uncover the truth and open their hearts?

Find out in the first installment:

COWBOY SWAGGER

Available September 2010

Look for more
SONS OF TROY LEDGER
stories coming soon!

www.eHarlequin.com

HI69495